Naked to Naked Goes

Naked to Naked Goes

STORIES BY

ROBERT FLANAGAN

CHARLES SCRIBNER'S SONS
NEW YORK
1986

Library of Congress Cataloging-in-Publication Data

Flanagan, Robert, 1941-
  Naked to naked goes.

  I. Title.
PS3556.L34N3   1986   813'.54   85-27891
ISBN 0-684-18671-3

Published simultaneously in Canada
by Collier Macmillan Canada, Inc.

Composition by Maryland Linotype

Manufactured by Fairfield Graphics

Designed by Marek Antoniak

First Edition

With love, first and always, for Katy;
and for good friends, critics, and storytellers:
Michael Harrah, Henry J. Leuchter, and Scott Sommer.

Contents

Acknowledgments

The following stories appeared in these periodicals: "Berzerk" in *Chicago* magazine; "Close Dancing" in *Orpheus*; "Gaming" in *Fiction*; "Naked to Naked Goes" in *The Ohio Review*; "Smoker" in *Chromium 16*.

"Gaming" also appeared in *Three Times Three*, a short-fiction collection published by Court Street Chapbooks, Ithaca, NY.

And I wish to thank the National Endowment for the Arts and the Ohio Arts Council for their generous support, and Ohio Wesleyan University for time off from teaching in order to write.

Love and War are the same thing,
and stratagems and policy are as allowable in the one
as in the other.

—Cervantes

Naked to Naked Goes

Come morning his split lip is as purple as a nightcrawler stuck on a hook. Steam from his shower makes the window's gray November light watery. Stiff from his brief, cramped sleep on the couch, he splashes cold water in his face, eyes grainy and lips stinging, before retreating from the fogged mirror.

When he puts on his glasses, the lenses appear blurred. He wipes them on his robe. The blur remains. His present vision dizzies him at times. His optician advises him that his next prescription will be bifocals.

He pauses before the bedroom door. Once before when she locked him out, he kicked it open. They were much younger then though, and not nearly as familiar as they are now with the script they have chosen for their lives. Then, he stood by the splintered jamb and actually shouted "Don't you *ever* lock me out!" As he recalls it, he felt uneasy even as he spoke; he sounded a bit too much like Robert Mitchum, kingfish of some small southern town, warning his new bride (Deborah Kerr?): "There'll be no locked doors between us."

Beyond the varnished plane he hears the white silence of his wife's anger. The screws to the lock, reset in wood putty, would give more easily now, but he'd need to feel a purer sense of outrage than he does to kick them into giving. At forty, he seems to have outgrown purity.

Yet his dreams and fantasies deny his age. They return him to his teens, or earlier. What woke him this morning was a dream he repeatedly suffered in the stage between bed-wetting and masturbation: he was a thumb on the edge of the world, exposed and fragile, and the round earth was whirling at tremendous speed. He knew he would either fall off or, in a near collision of planets, be snapped off to go hurtling through space, cold and utterly separate.

He passes his daughter's room. Hanging from the doorknob is a *Do Not Disturb* motel tag he brought back from a business trip. In the middle of the door, in Magic Marker Baroque, a placard warns *Knock Before Entering. This Means You!* When she was small she wanted her door open at night; she wanted Mommy's and Daddy's door open too. When they closed it some nights, she was hurt. Now her door is closed day and night. She's discovered the power she holds in common with adults. She can deny others entrance.

When her radio-alarm bursts into rock, she will slap it silent. He or his wife will have to drag her from bed and walk her about as though she were drunk. She sleeps so much it worries him. When he was a teenager sleep was his cocoon, his retreat from a world which demanded that he act both as child and adult. And, although he's not certain about his daughter's situation, for him bed was also the place to be alone with the new excitement and shame his changing body offered.

A week ago his daughter suffered, or celebrated, her first period. She did not want him to know. His wife told him but told him not to tell her. "She'll let you know when she's ready." So he and his daughter carry their secrets about the house as if balancing eggs on their heads.

He opens the door to the third bedroom. The room was intended for their second child (second of four: two boys, two girls), an aspiration that expired in the course of his wife's miscarriages.

A gleaming chromium hospital bed holds what is left of his mother. She lies still, either sleeping or dead. For his sake this morning, with the long night a load on his heart and his head's blood drumming, he hopes she's sleeping; for her sake he hopes she's dead. He stands at the door, but cannot summon up the courage to enter.

He goes down the hall. The house is a single story frame ranch. They put a down payment on it thirteen years ago as a temporary home. It would be too small for them in the long run, they thought then, but time proved them wrong.

In the kitchen he loads the percolator. Most mornings at this time he'd just be returning from his run, eager for a shower, anticipating the day. Now the muddy white Nikes dangling from the basement doorknob seem artifacts from another life. The water in the percolator begins pumping, like a heart, begins darkening.

He has eggs and toast on plates when his wife appears. Usually she serves breakfast in her robe and slippers; now she sits at the table in a dark green skirt and yellow jersey and reads the morning paper. Her earrings are jade teardrops. Her hair is long and black, skin olive, upper lip shaded by fuzz. Her grandfather came from Sicily. Like her brothers, who load and drive the family's produce trucks, she looks as firm and healthy as a melon.

Poking at his eggs, he downs three cups of black coffee. He stares at the bra straps constraining her flesh. This is the third day of their estrangement. It began over something trivial—which one of them forgot to turn on the crock-pot—but actually grew from the fatigue of watching over his mother, and from the futility felt living close to death. What good *is* love if it does nothing to ease the pain of dying? What does a relationship mean, even a blood one, when pain and pills erase all recognition of it? These are his questions, he realizes, but he thinks his wife must ask them as well.

He holds his cooling cup and does not speak.

"You'll be late," she says, finally.

"I'm not going in."

"Sick?"

"Why don't you take the day for yourself. Do some shopping."

"Your penance?"

"You ought to have a break sometime."

"Was that what last night was, your break?"

He sips his coffee. "I suppose."

"And just what was it, your break?" Although her tone is casual, he senses the hook concealed in the question. They had this all out five years ago; she said she would never stand for it again and he believes her.

"I drove around."

"Is that how you hurt yourself?"

"No." Abruptly clear, the memory is there. "I got in a fight," he says with unfeigned surprise.

"You *what*?"

He shrugs. In a bar's narrow gravel lot a drunk passed a remark which he did not, as he would have had he been alone, let go unnoticed. The scuffle ended with the battling males falling away from each other; he had a split lip, the other a bloody nose. He'd retrieved his glasses and walked away, his shoulderblades lifting in expectation of a gunshot which did not come. The girl on his arm said he was brave. There was no mockery in her voice; she was just too young to know better. "I was drinking," he says.

"I could smell that."

"I'm sorry. I really am."

In her eyes the questions show clearly, as well as her need not to have them answered. Who wants the truth if all the truth offers is pain?

"Did you check on Mom?"

He nods.

Their daughter drags into the room. She is as tall as her mother now and the breasts poking up the "Grateful Dead" T-shirt are more than bumps amusing her parents. He remembers holding her on his lap in her pink sleepers, "Bye Baby Bunting, Daddy's gone a-hunting." When she was two he read her her favorite story, "Ant and Bee," a beginning alphabet book, so many times that he knows it by heart.

> *Bee* and *Ant* wanted to go and live
> with a spider friend who lived
> in a
> ### WEB
> The *web* was very comfortable
> and their spider friend did not
> mind if *ant* and *bee* lived with
> him in his *web*.
> *Bee* and *ant* waved goodbye to
> *dog* and *man* and blew lots of
> ### XXX
> *XXX* means kisses if you draw
> them on paper.

If he reminded her of that now, she would "*totally die!*"

"I'll drop you at school," his wife tells their daughter.

At the door he pats his wife's shoulder, but attempts nothing more. He wishes that his gift to her of a free day were untainted by guilt. He feels enormously grateful to her for the way she's cared for his mother. In fact it often seems to him that she's closer to his mother, as woman to woman, than he is as her son.

Bulky with books, his daughter brushes by. She puckers him a kiss at a range of two feet, "Mmm!," then clops down the porch steps in her impractical clogs.

"I don't know when I'll be back," his wife says.

He listens for *or if*.

At nine he calls his office. He informs his secretary that for today the firm must publicly relate the concerns of glass manufacture and the hygienic benefits of pure glass containers without his able and creative direction. She accepts the message, her voice giving no indication of amusement. He almost asks her is she all right (Meaning is she angry with him? Meaning how does *she* feel about the situation?), but knows that other secretaries are near her desk, bright and trim young women adorned for work with thin gold necklaces and coral lip gloss and coral fingernail polish, and so asks instead if she will please cancel his appointments. She agrees to do so, her voice unrelentingly that of the secretary speaking in the line of duty to the temporarily indisposed editor of the house organ. "I *am* the house organ," he'd shouted last night and she had laughed as though he were truly clever. He is slightly disappointed, but largely relieved, that her voice betrays no intimacy.

He hangs up, his apologies unspoken. The tone of her voice informed him that she needs distance as much as he does. He thinks he understands. She told him, candidly, that her secretary's job is temporary. Come summer, she's off to L.A. where a "friend" is willing to put her up. She's involved in a relationship now, she said, but nothing really serious. She's not going to make the mistake again of jumping into marriage; that, she says, was a "real mind bender—a real fantasyland."

At her apartment, drunkenly sorting through her record collection, waiting until it seemed right to reach for her, he understood just how badly out of place he was: "Do Ya Think I'm Sexy" and "Hit Me With Your Best Shot." He recalls his father, while shaving, singing "I give it to you and you give it to me, true love." Now, the times seem a tuning fork struck by moral revolution and humming with sexual vibration.

He folds his long body onto the couch. Last night echoes in his temples. Stopping at taverns, driving at eighty and ninety miles an hour over narrow country roads, singing and shouting in the confines of the family wagon, he did not know exactly what he was hunting, but he knew he was hunting some kind of explosive escape, some craziness to release the bending pressure. Then the chance meeting (which was not truly a chance meeting, because he recalls having heard the office girls mention the bar as one they liked) that provided a release safer than some others.

"You look so *worried*," she said. And later, "I have some Scotch at my place." In bed she behaved as if her young body were a yo-yo or Frisbee, a bright and simple toy, offering for his enjoyment its tricks and possibilities, surfaces and surprises. He enjoyed her. In flickering candlelight he provided from the depth of his drunkenness a secret erect center upon which her slim form rose and fell and turned as he, like a potter with clay, stroked crevice and curve with his fingertips.

Even then he was not overcome with passion. He felt that he might at any moment disengage to politely offer his gratitude and regrets and return to his established life. Not that the girl wasn't attractive. Her conical, unnursed breasts were so perfect they seemed a retouched photograph. Yet despite the testimony of skin and eye, and the power of imagination to present his experience to him even at the moment that it was happening as an exotic and exciting scene in which any man in his right body would yearn to participate, even then his mind refused to do other than pronounce the hard truth that what he felt was not desire, but only its derivative: desire for desire.

In the office her skirts and blouses defined her slim suppleness; in bed he was struck by the fleshy weight of her buttocks. His wife, appearing overly ripe in skirt and sweater, in the nude felt surprisingly compact. It seemed to him in his limited experience that women, naked, were more alike than distinct, were less individual than limited variations on a perfect form.

He goes to his desk where he makes an effort to balance the checkbook, poking the calculator buttons with the eraser end of a pencil. Money comes in and goes out. Subtraction outpaces addition. A corner of his desk is chipped.

In fifteen years of marriage he has twice been unfaithful to his wife, the first time over five years ago. That time was more serious; he'd been with the woman five or six times (in truth, seven) over the span of a month. That he broke off with her, and that last night he was so drunk he could not complete his part of the act, do not, he supposes, make his actions less unfaithful.

Nor is he much comforted by computing his fidelity rating on a yearly basis as a positive 86 percent, or on a daily basis his infidelity rating (eight days out of 5,478) as a minuscule .146 percent.

When he told his first other woman that he would not be seeing her again, her hysterical anger burst over him like a breaking wave. If he broke off with her, he was nothing but a hypocrite. He denied it at the time, but later came to admit the charge. Seen from the inside, however, a hypocrite is someone too weak to consistently act in accordance with his beliefs, yet too strong to deny the validity of those beliefs in order to vindicate his weakness.

He goes up the hall to stand beside the hospital bed and look down as though from a dizzying height at the shallowly breathing, emaciated form. If he'd not been witness to the cancer's progress, he would not now recognize this skeletal, straw-haired figure as his mother. "Mom?"

One eye opens, blurred and filmed, reptilian.

"I'll get you something. I'll be right back."

He comes back from the kitchen with a cup of beef bouillon, a glass of water and her morning pain pills. His mother is staring at the ceiling. One bony hand picks at nothing. He kisses her cheek, her flesh as dry as papier-mâché. Her eye takes him in without apparent recognition; again he is chilled by that blank look.

He lifts her to a sitting position with his left arm. She has no more weight than a two-suiter bag. When he touches her she doesn't cry out, because the night's medication has not yet worn off. He gives her the new pills and water, then holds the warm mug to her lips. She sucks in bouillon. He feels guilty in urging nourishment upon her, as he knows she wants nothing to prolong the pain. More than once when he's sat up with her at night, she's whispered, "Kill me, kill me!" tears sliding down from her arid cheeks. (And he hears a voice from his past: The Experienced Woman hissing, "Fuck me, fuck me!") Or his mother had suddenly turned hard-eyed and crafty, asking him, "Who are you?" And as suddenly, "Leave all the pills with me. No one will know."

One night he did leave a new bottle of Talwin on her nightstand. Later he started from sleep thinking it was a dream. He hurried to her room. The bottle was untouched and his mother was sleeping, her breathing like sandpaper on stone. He could not tell for certain just what had been his intentions, or precisely what he felt at retrieving the bottle.

"Do you have to get up?" He lifts her from the bed and manages to place her on the portable commode. She brushes his hands away to claw up her nightgown; he catches a glimpse of the slack, hanging thighs before her hands grasp the commode's side rails and he can safely look away.

When he was a boy and they put his father, after his breakdown, in the Veterans Home, she took a job to support the two of them. He would hold onto a favorite dress of hers and kiss it and cry into it when she left for work, even though the woman next door who was watching him said he ought to be ashamed of himself. He thinks he was four or five at the time, and he's not certain if he remembers holding the dress or only remembers being told about it. His mother worked the three to eleven shift as a plug tamper making five thousand Champion spark plugs a night. He would sit with her at the kitchen table before her ride came, watching her cut the strips of gray tape and line them up on the table's edge, then one by one layer with tape the tips of her fingers to protect them from the newly tooled steel of the plugs. He thought she was every bit as brave as the boxers he watched with his uncles on the Gillette Friday Night Fights. But he wasn't brave. He cried in her dress the minute she left.

He hears urine trickling into the commode. It sounds like rain from a gutter, like glucose in I.V. tubes, like rivulets of blood from a vampire's bite, like time.

When his daughter bangs on the front door, he opens it and stands back as she dashes past him to the bathroom. He does not know if it's trouble with her period or if she still hates to use the school toilets, and he doesn't ask.

She rushes from the bathroom to the refrigerator, grabs an apple and heads for the back door. "Auditions!" she announces. "I don't know what time ..."

He surprises them both by clasping her shoulders and awkwardly kissing her on the forehead.

"Daddy!" she giggles, bites the apple, and leaves.

He gives his mother her medication a half hour before the previous dose is timed to wear off. He realizes that he ought to wait the full four hours between doses, that otherwise he keeps throwing off the schedule, yet he cannot bear to see her suffer unnecessary pain. It's not as though she is going to recover and need to withdraw from drug dependence. She's a terminal case. All he can do until she dies is to keep her from feeling too keenly the pain of living.

At five he moves fish sticks from freezer to oven and warms canned green beans on the range. At six he and his daughter eat supper in the kitchen. He says her mother is still shopping. "All this time!" his daughter exclaims. "God!" She picks at the beans; they are "gross." She describes the part in the high school play she is positively sure to get, not the lead but still "a really super part." It relieves him to see her so animated, and does not trouble him that she no longer asks how her grandmother is. She *knows* how her grandmother is and knows there is nothing she can do about it.

When his daughter goes to her room to study, he phones his secretary at her apartment. "I just thought I'd call."

"Hey, it's okay. It's no big thing, you know."

"I know," he says. "Okay."

He phones his sister-in-law to ask if his wife is there.

"Why should she be here?"

"Is she?"

"You haven't lost her, have you?"

The lack of alarm in her voice tells him what he wants to know. "I just want to be sure she's okay."

After sitting with his mother for a time and making sure she swallows her night medication, he goes to his bedroom. His wife's white nightgown dangles from a hook on the inside of the closet door. On his desk at the office is a framed photograph of her in white bridal gown, her broad smile fierce in its energy and confidence, her black hair glittering like obsidian. He touches the slack gown. He knows her body almost as well as his own, and can clearly picture her veined breasts, padded thighs, and belly traced with stretch marks.

He traced his secretary's appendix scar with an index finger. The woman who called him a hypocrite once thrust at him both upturned wrists to bare silvery crescents she claimed her ex-husband's cruelty caused her. His daughter wears a half-inch scar over her left eyebrow, the result of a fall when he was teaching her to ride a two-wheeler.

He strips, lays his glasses on the dresser, and drops to the floor to do push-ups and sit-ups. In college, before he discovered theater, he wrestled at 150 pounds. Although he won more than he lost, he was never outstanding. His coach urged him to forget all else but wrestling, claiming it was the best preparation for life he could ever have. He doubted his coach then, and knows now the man was mistaken. Life's conflicts did not respect weight class. You went up against everything from 118 pounds to heavyweights and the open-ended periods stretched far beyond your second wind.

After deep knee bends, he slips on pajama bottoms and steps across the hall to his daughter's room. He has to bang a fist against the door to be heard over her radio. When she opens the door, he says "Bedtime."

She sighs heavily. "Daddy!"

"Now," he says.

"Where's Mom?" She insolently cocks her hip, an accusation.

"She's visiting your aunt."

Her eyebrows lift. She knows what goes on.

"So what happened to your lip?"

"I fell."

"Oh, sure."

"Goodnight," he says.

"I don't see why I have to go to bed when I'm not even tired. I'm almost grown up, you know. I mean, I'm menstruating and all."

"You are?" He smiles. "How about that. Congratulations."

"Come on, you knew."

"How would I know? Well, you're growing up. That's good, you're doing fine. I'm proud of you."

Just for a moment her look is unguarded and he spies the trusting inquisitive child behind the teen's mask of isolated indifference.

"So I get to stay up, right?"

"No." He pats her shoulder. "Bedtime."

She sighs and closes her door.

He checks on his mother, then gets into bed, opening *The Nez Percé Campaign*, a history of Chief Joseph's brilliant, but failed, strategic retreat. He has trouble focusing on the text.

Hanging on the wall before him is a framed print of Van Gogh's "Reclining Female Nude." The full-fleshed naked woman lies on what he imagines to be a canopied bed, facing away, her head resting on one bare arm. Her face is hidden, a secret despite her nakedness. The visible ear is a red portal, as though something has caused the blood to rush to her head. Her long dark hair hangs in a loosened braid down the fawn hillsides of her shoulders. There is a deep crease in the flesh of her bent waist, a reddish tint running down her spine to become bright red flecks —he wonders if it's blood—at the spine's base and buttocks' crease. Her left, upper buttock is an oval of creamy light. Massive thighs taper to girlish calves and small feet, the toes curling as though in the aftermath of ecstasy.

He puts down his book and picks up the bedside telephone, a white Princess model, then puts that down too.

Staring at the Van Gogh, he cautions himself against being overly romantic. For many men women are no more than acquisitions, necessary luxuries to be financed on time, the various models and years to be compared with each other in regard to features and performance. At the Racquet Club, he and other desk-confined men slip out of suits and ties to don jocks, shorts, and tribal headbands. Often, as they work on leather gloves for a firmer grip on the court's steel weaponry, the remarks come. "Hear you got a new secretary?" "Haven't *got* her yet, give me a week or two." "You catch the coffee shop girl? Got an ass that'll break your heart!"

It was worse in the army. The lunch-hour athletes return at night to the qualifying presence of women. When all a man had to return to was a barracks filled with men, even if the return was from the brief relief provided by an antiseptic-scented prostitute, there was nothing to take the edge from the talk. A soldier was leaving his wife because "the fucking I'm getting ain't worth the fucking I'm getting." A sergeant explained that when God dealt the cards "he gave women all four aces right between the legs." The only way to come on to a broad was to come on strong. If she said "no" she meant "yes." If she really meant "no" then the bitch deserved what she got. You ever let a woman get the best of you, you were pussy-whipped, you were as good as dead.

In the confines of the long spare barracks and chain-fenced camp, sex was war. Casualties were men who got "Dear John" letters or a dose of clap, fatalities were those who got married. "Why buy the cow when you can get the milk for free?" Sometimes the men won guerrilla actions—a whore wasn't paid, a discharged trooper deserted his wife, a bar-girl was gotten drunk and forced to serve a squad—but surely they were losing the war.

The telephone rings. He seizes the receiver. A husky, squeaky voice asks to speak to his daughter. He say that she can't come to the phone at the moment and asks if he may take a message. "Ah," the voice says, then "Uh-uh," and is followed by a click.

Being born male seemed to make one a member of a warlike tribe, regardless of any desire to join. He often felt like a traitor to his tribe. He was the one who drove the bar-girl from the barracks back to town and, though he hadn't used her, gave her the two tens from his wallet. "The bastards!" she kept saying. "The bastards." On liberty once, seeing a sailor slap a woman's face, he automatically hit him. The sailor was drunk and sat down hard in a gutter, cupping his jaw. "Jesus-fucking-Christ!" he wailed. "She's a whore, man. Whose side you on here?"

Nothing in the locker room or barracks talk ever touched on the mystery of women. Either the talkers thought there was no mystery or if there once was it had long been solved. He did not venture to bring up the subjects of lunar tides and menstrual cycles, or man's fascination with the virgin/whore, or how Rodin's Pygmalion and Galatea were joined at the base in marble from which they had not yet fully emerged or into which they were merging, or the beyond-logic experience a man had of returning to wholeness when a woman willingly made of herself a safe harbor for him. He held his silence lest someone look at him oddly and say what it all boiled down to was a man had to stick it in something. Like the others, he picked up his racquet and went to the court to whack like mad his little blue balls against the flat white walls. Like the others, he acted as though the mystery he lived with and to which he put a common name was a mystery only to the young and inexperienced and that it was foolish for a grown man to waste time considering it.

He snaps off the light and turns toward the empty space created by his wife's absence.

Men ought not to be judged too harshly. Any man knows, although quick to deny it, that it's in self-protection he puffs and struts his fantasized power. A man knows that lacking a woman he becomes a useless dangling, and that loving a woman he becomes vulnerable.

As always in the first few moments of letting the day slide toward sleep, he experiences an unsettling sensation of floating. He places a hand on his wife's pillow.

The first woman (or girl, for she was no older than his daughter is now) he saw naked lived in his neighborhood and played ball and tag with him. One night she phoned him to come to her house. When he got there, she was alone and wearing a robe and he asked what she wanted. She went into her parents' bedroom, then called him. He stepped into the room and stopped cold. She was naked. An overhead light shone directly down on her. She was plump, nearly fat, and he could barely believe that any body could be so smooth-skinned and rounded. His skin was prickly and pimply, scabbed and bruised, his bones hard and near the surface. The girl took his cold hand and placed it on the warm, soft oval of one breast. He just stood there, holding her and looking away, until she laughed and said, "Oh, you!" and grabbed her robe. Returned to his room, biting his pillow and stroking himself, he wished so hard he thought his heart might stop that he'd had the nerve to move his hand and touch her *there.* He feared he'd never again have the chance to do it. And he didn't with her.

Turning onto his back, he slides both hands beneath his head. A streetlamp casts a wedge of light on the ceiling. During his junior year in college, entranced by Bergson's *Time and Free Will* and frustrated by Kantian categories, he became entranced and frustrated by a Japanese-American girl, a music major and violinist who played in the orchestra for the run of "Fiddler on the Roof," in which he was cast as the radical student.

He admired the violinist from a distance. At the time he was involved with a divorced woman, a tall, horsey blonde only a year older than he, although he was two years older than most of his classmates as a result of his time in the army, who conceived of herself as The Experienced Woman. She was a psychology major. She treated him, the Army Vet, as though he were The Experienced Man, and he did his utmost to act the part although he suspected at times that she was only enjoying the irony of his miscasting. The divorcee had her own apartment, its glass bathroom shelves stocked with decanters of bath powers and tubes of body ointments, and wore underthings from Fredericks of Hollywood. She would touch $50-an-ounce perfume to her earlobes and to the valley between her breasts, the gesture characterized by a sense of reverence, as though she were offering incense to a divinity.

"You're so smart," she would say, reading one of his philosophy papers, or "You're so strong," cradled in his arms, or "Fuck me, fuck me," her legs over his shoulders and body bent so far back he feared he would snap her in two.

He wanted to believe that he loved her and that theirs was a grand passion. Yet, despite her fierce claims of how much she needed him, there was always something impersonal about her lovemaking. And although he tried not to think about it, he really didn't like her very much. Her comments about psychology were clinical and tedious, she had no interest in theater, despite her theatricality, and to his dismay she was unashamed of voting Republican. Yet he could not keep his hands off her. When she reached her climax, she tossed back her head, the veins in her long neck standing out, eyes squeezed shut, teeth clenched, her tanned body going stone-still except for a fluttering in her flat blonde-fuzzed belly. "Oh Jesus!" she would hiss, her breath like steam. "Jesus Christ, I thought I'd *die!*"

He knew full well that there were hundreds of men who'd cut off an ear to be in his shoes, in her pants. And yet.

One night on impulse he did not call her after he finished his "Fiddler" performance. He asked the violinist out for a drink. She didn't drink, so they had coffee at a Big Boy. They had coffee together three nights running. In the green room she played her violin for him, "The Lark Ascending," with such clarity and grace that he was moved to tears. When she saw his reaction, she kissed him. He tried to hold her, but she held him off. She said that she would like to be his good friend.

It was a month after he began dating the violinist, at a time when he was beginning to think that he really ought to call The Experienced Woman to see how she was doing (After all, they'd had *something* together, hadn't they? And what if something had happened to her? He hadn't seen her on campus for weeks), that he heard the blonde had run off to California with an assistant professor of psychology.

"Why would he leave his family and job like that?" another student wondered.

He passed on the tribal wisdom of his sergeants. "A stiff prick knows no conscience."

He courted the violinist for six months. When she played for him, when certain remarks of his made her cast down her almond eyes, when he held her hand in his, when he touched her luminous black hair, he felt certain that he was in love with her.

"There are things best left unconsummated," she told him, the formality of her diction distancing him more effectively than her small hand on his chest. She was not interested in marriage for many years to come because of her career; she might love him but she would not be his lover. In his best seminar-trained logic, he explained that what they were confronting was the difference between the idealist and the humanist. The idealist preferred the perfect form over a marred, but realizable approximation; the humanist chose flawed reality, and might even deface attempts at formal perfection in the name of humanity, hence the prevalence of graffiti on statues and the scrawled names and dates in fresh cement . . . Goddamit, he exclaimed, didn't she realize she had a body?

If he were an artist, she said, he would understand.

After a time, they stopped seeing each other. For a few years they exchanged letters and Christmas cards, and then occasionally she would send him concert programs. The last program he received from her came from San Francisco, years ago. Still, every so often, seeing a stretch of fresh cement, admiring the far pearl of a winter storm, or waxing his car, he will imagine he hears a violin singing, and in his mind's eyes the lark ascends.

He glances at the headboard shelf where the radio's digital read-out displays 11:12. He's not aware of staring until he sees 11:13. The flick of the minutes unnerves him, and he blinds his eyes with his wife's pillow. He regrets the loss of the old round-faced alarm with its relentless but smooth second hand sweep presenting time as a continuity to be lived in, like a river to be floated, rather than time as a series of electric segments with one's life a fitful dance to strobe lights.

The woman with him rises from bed and he says sleepily, "Just leave your body here." He tells her he wants it for company, so he won't get cold. But he's excited by the possibility of being alone with her body so he can freely explore it, turning it this

19

way and that, touching and looking, with no concern for her mind or feelings, and with no danger of his eyes meeting hers.

The digital clock reads 12:01. He gets out of bed and goes to the living room, discounting his dream as the result of nerves. Sagging in an armchair, he watches the television with the sound off. "Night Owl Theatre" offers the adventures of a specially chosen U.S. team parachuted behind enemy lines to blow up a Nazi-held castle. The team contains the standard male types: the brutal but effective killer, the spit and polish officer, the black market hustler, the lover boy, and the secret coward who will crack in early action but redeem himself at the film's climax by getting machine-gunned while covering the survivors' escape. He has seen this film, or others like it, dozens of times. They form the bulk of late night offerings. The programmers know who's sleepless and in need of fantasy heroics.

When he and his wife had been married less than a year, he went off for his fourth and final army reserve summer camp, two weeks of marching on red clay roads and humping about pine barrens playing at war. And day in and day out hearing the tribal chants.

On the march: I got a gal in Tijuana, she knows how but she don't wanna.

At the latrine: Looka here, it's Needle Dick, the bug fucker.

During chow: What this old boy's hungry for is some taint meat. That little piece in between.—T'aint pussy, t'aint ass.

In the barracks: Know a girl back home who'd screw a rock pile, she thought there was a snake under it.

On guard: Sure you married, boy. You married to Rosey Palm.

Of course he knew it was all bullshit; it was all whistling in the dark. (Q: What's the difference between dark and hard? A: It stays dark all night.) Of course it didn't touch him or his real life.

And yet, picked up at the reserve center on his return, his wife delighted to see him and filled with plans for an evening of dinner and dancing, he drove to a park and coerced her into making love to him. It wasn't exactly rape, but it wasn't play either. "Don't, please." But he did. "Not here." But he did it in the car's back seat, frenzied in a tangle of underwear. Even when she cried out that he was hurting her, it added to his excitement. The hurt meant he was big enough; better yet, too big. Although later of course the memory would make him feel terribly small, and ashamed. Later he would be quiet and deferential about the apartment, pained by the searching looks she gave him.

Even now, after fifteen years together, she does not seem too certain of him. And rightfully so. He tries to maintain his balance and generally succeeds. He helps his wife with the housework and cooking, his daughter with her homework and growing up, his mother with her slow dying. He regularly goes to work, pays the family bills on time, changes the station wagon's spark plugs and oil, cleans the gutters, repairs screens, mows and rakes the lawn, shovels snow, orders flowers sent home on no occasion other than a sudden brimming of his heart. He doesn't smoke, drinks only sporadically, jogs daily.

Yet come her period, a full moon, or an argument and he can feel the hair on his head getting thicker, his hands heavier . . . What gets thicker and heavier is his cock, or so it seems; what brain he possesses shrinks until it becomes easier to ignore than the dangling hot weight of his balls. So full of need, and angered by feeling so needy, he suddenly argues about anything, slams the door to go for hard, fast drives, sleeps on the couch as if to illustrate his bitter isolation.

"What do you want from me?" she'll cry out at the peak of an argument. And he won't answer or will only pretend to answer. What does he want? He wants to be excited and to be exciting. He wants to know that although they are dying they aren't dead yet. He wants to escape into softness under the pretense of manly exploration, to surrender himself while appearing to dominate. "What does any man want?" he'll shout in response, putting the blame on her as he puts a door between them.

He turns off the television and sits at his desk, switching on a tensor lamp, to sift through canceled check stubs. Opening his briefcase, he spends the better part of an hour doodling with a pencil as he tries to think of a clever way to relate the public benefits of his firm's new two-liter bottle. He sketches bottles and links them with graceful loops, picturing in his mind the silicate and soda fused by fire and the formed glass shaped into various containers of brittle strength and bright transparency.

A photo cube holds snapshots of his parents, his wife and daughter on a picnic, a baby picture of his daughter, and one of his wife as she appeared when they were first dating.

He loves her. He fears that his slip with the secretary will drive a wedge between them; the other time did. Wedge by wedge they might be driven apart until there remained no possibility for the natural grain of their love to mend itself. He is afraid they might wane into still another prematurely old couple seated at bay in overstuffed chairs in an outmoded living room, passing their days barely speaking and their nights in separate beds, figures rendered so glassy-eyed and stiff-fleshed by the truce of their lives that they appear to have been prepared by a taxidermist for display in a museum of failed hopes.

What if she didn't come back? He's imagined her sleeping at her sister's place, taking a needed break before returning, but for all he knows she and her sister, nervy from coffee, are reciting in harmony a litany of male abuse. Her sister divorced her patrolman husband, who would leave home on his evenings off to get the car washed and be gone for hours, and joined a women's consciousness group. He's heard her speeches. She vows never to remarry. No man is to be trusted, she claims, and no man is worth the trouble it takes to keep him happy. Even a lover is too much trouble. Celibacy, she's learned, is freedom. A stiff conscience knows no prick, he once told her, earning her enmity.

If his sister-in-law talks his wife into filing for divorce, he will fight it. Perhaps he'll be able to prove by the fierceness of his fight the love he's failed to demonstrate clearly in their daily life.

Unless she's given up on him; unless she just doesn't care anymore.

He recalls one night when they went to a little Italian restaurant she loved; he sat listening with one ear to her talk about the art gallery where she worked part-time, catching what he could of the intense, whispered conversation of the couple at the next table. Overhearing the word "divorce," he'd perked up his ears as though someone had mentioned a trip to Shanghai or Tierra Del Fuego, some exotic locale he might like to visit. The man looked to be in his mid-forties; the woman, although most likely the same age, had not weathered as well and clearly appeared fifty. "I thought we'd grow old together," she said, her voice breaking. "I thought we did," the man replied. The remainder of the meal the couple maintained silence. The man wasn't about to be stuck in a museum. Yet where did he think he was headed? Out of the old orbit into one of his own, yes, but into what cold and empty stretches of space? Into some form of suspended animation? Would he evolve into one of those aging swingers with their gold ID bracelets and disco chains, creaking their bodies into wing-doored sports cars, the dry wrinkles about their fear-sparked eyes like the etchings of desert erosion?

He dials his sister-in-law's number. After a dozen rings, he hangs up.

He fears his wife's anger. A man might blow up and make a lot of noise, but mostly he was bluffing and knew when to call it quits. A woman, especially when she was hurt, might do anything. When she felt she was in the right, his wife was like a stone wall.

He had met her at a college dance, shortly after breaking off with the violinist. She wore a long white dress and had her black hair done in two thin braids to sweep up in a crown to knot at the back of her head, the rest of her hair falling free. She looked very striking. He asked her to dance and, afterwards, sat at her table. She was a humanities major, four years younger than he.

They dated for over a month before he tried to make love to her. She refused.

"Virginity is not all that precious," he said, The Experienced Man. "Especially not if it gets in the way of life."

"This is life right now," she replied, "even if we do still have our clothes on." She added: "I didn't say I was a virgin."

"No, you didn't *say* it." He allowed himself a knowing smile. "And I'm not."

"Oh." He nodded. Because she was Catholic and her family Sicilian, he guessed he'd just assumed. And because she stopped his hands whenever they began to roam. "Well, you certainly don't owe me any explanation," he said in a tone of hurt resignation which of course drew out an explanation: a high school boyfriend, a reaction against her family.

"Whatever happened to him?" He wanted to ask, "Was he the only one?"

"I don't know. We broke up."

After a discreet interval during which he thought he showed himself to be mature and considerate, he again tried to make love to her and again was rebuffed. "But why?"

"Because I don't want to. No, that's not true. Because I don't choose to, not now."

"*Now* is all we ever have."

She looked at him, disappointment showing in her eyes. "You think," she said, "that because I made, because I've been fucked . . ."

"Don't."

"Because I've been fucked before I ought to let you fuck me now. You have a very simple mind, that's your problem."

He did not call her for a week. He saw her on campus and passed by without speaking.

He did not call her for a month. He saw her at a Chopin recital and asked her to have a drink with him afterwards, but she refused.

A few days after the recital the mail brought an envelope addressed to him in her handwriting. He tore it open. It held a 3x5 card:

> I gave what other women gave
> That stepped out of their clothes,
> But when the soul, its body off,

> Naked to naked goes,
> He it has found shall find therein
> What none other knows.

He recognized the lines as coming from Yeats, but wasn't sure what they were supposed to tell him. She wouldn't make love to him *because* she loved him? He searched through Yeats and found the poem, a Crazy Jane piece, "A Last Confession." She confessed to him and found him unsympathetic and now would keep herself for someone more deserving?

He felt certain that he loved her. It was a feeling distinctly different from what he'd felt for either the divorcee or the violinist. It called on more of him; it touched all those parts of him he thought of as his self.

He answered her in kind, copying his message from Robert Graves' "Pygmalion to Galatea":

> As you are woman, so be lovely:
> As you are lovely, so be various;
> Merciful as constant, constant as various,
> So be mine, as I yours for ever.

The next day he wrote to her again. "That was a proposal. Please say yes."

His mother and daughter sleeping soundly, he puts on supporter, socks, and sweat suit, laces up his running shoes, and slips out the kitchen door.

There is no moon visible. Low smokey clouds hide the stars. He shuffles down the dark street, the chill air making his eyes water and lungs burn. Fatigue weights his legs, and he feels as though he is running in sand or knee-deep water.

In a carry-out lot two police cars are parked side by side, head to tail like horses in a field. High beams blazing, a truck clatters past him, emblazoned in red with his wife's maiden name, and loaded with produce.

At the turn for his three mile loop, he keeps going straight. His glasses fog over and he carries them in a hand, the streetlights becoming liquid streaks of white.

Extending his run has put him in the neighborhood, so he

turns into the winding avenue entering the development where his sister-in-law lives. The family wagon is parked beside his sister-in-law's white Fiesta. He breaks stride, walks to a cedar shake twinplex, and rings a doorbell.

He rings again. Finally, he leans on the bell.

His sister-in-law, wearing a robe, opens the door to the length of a short brass chain.

"I have to talk to her."

"When she wants to talk to you, she'll let you know."

"Let her tell me that."

"She'd be talking to you then, wouldn't she?" She puts all her disdain for him into a bitter grin. But he recognizes that she's not truly his enemy; she's just another of the walking wounded in the war between the sexes. He shouts for his wife.

"The cops'll be out here, you keep that up."

He shouts again. His sister-in-law glances behind her. He pounds a fist on the doorjamb.

"It's Stanley Kowalski," his sister-in-law says.

His wife's face appears in the crack. "What on earth do you think you're doing?"

"I want you to come home."

The sister-in-law is saying something. Whatever it is, the wife tells her "No."

Maybe his sister-in-law wants to call out her brothers: three beefy machos who would probably sympathize with him if he were their buddy in a bar ("You gotta show them who's boss, absolutely!"). But this is their baby sister who's the wife in question here, so out of family duty they'd have to toss his ass in the street and maybe teach him a few lessons in the proper respect for womanhood.

"You shouldn't leave your mother alone," his wife says.

"I'm going right back. Look, I'm really sorry; I love you. Get in the car, will you?"

"Call me tomorrow."

"I'm calling you now! What is it, you can't hear me?"

"Will you keep your voice down?"

He can see her sister watching them closely, as though she were a prison matron keeping an eye peeled on visitor's day. "Come home."

"You're too loud. You better go on."

"Are you coming home or not?" He cocks his head to one side to shout at his sister-in-law. "I want my wife back!"

"Will you stop," his wife says. "You don't live here, you . . ."

"Neither do you." His right thigh cramps and he dips quickly in a knee bend, then leans forward with his hands on the door and heels flat to the ground to stretch his hamstrings. Her face is inches from his. "I'm sorry about that time after reserve camp," he says, "and about kicking in the door. You sorry for locking me out? You sorry for not being there sometimes when I needed you so bad I felt like I'd break in half? What are we, some typical little suburban couple now, like those idiots on TV? All we ever argue about is whether to have cornflakes or grape nuts for breakfast, right? No, no, don't close the door. You owe it to me to hear me out. I want to know—what's it going to be, you going to leave me because I'm not perfect, because sometimes I get fucked up like anybody else who's got a real life? You just going to pack up and walk out, black and white, pure and simple? And you think that's not simpleminded?

Her eyes shine with tears. He presses against the crack in the door until he can almost kiss her. "Have you forgotten how it was when we were going together? We had rough times then, we knew it wasn't all going to be picture perfect. You remember your Yeats? Crazy Jane talking to the bishop, you remember that? 'Love has pitched his mansion in the place of excrement, for nothing can be sole or whole that has not been rent.' Or is that too corny for us now, huh? Is that it?"

He steps back and waits for her to speak. She closes the door.

"Okay," he says. He backs to the street, then turns and runs away from the development, running hard in the littered gutter, heels hitting heavily, cold hands balled into fists. He struggles to control his breathing, sucking air in deep through his nose and letting it explode from his mouth. His lungs give out before his legs. He slows to a stumbling jog, then a walk, gasping and hawking strings of spit.

He limps back to his house and strips in the bathroom, his heart pumping so hard it thuds in his ears. He eyes his body in the mirror as though it might belong to an enemy. His stomach is flat, but his arms appear brittle and pale in the overhead light. His thighs twitch as though shot through with electricity. The mirror begins to fog from his body heat. He towels off, wraps a dry towel about his waist, and wanders into the dark living room.

A sudden thump, heavy and single, stills him. He puts a hand to his chest, awaiting the pain, then with relief places the sound outside his heart.

His mother's room is dark, but he hears movement and switches on the light. She is on the floor, curled on one side, her fingers moving like feelers. Her gown is pulled up about her shriveled thighs. The portable commode has been tipped over and urine stains the carpet.

He grasps her beneath the arms. "You're hurting me." He lifts her as gently as he can, hugging her frail body to him. Her gown is soaked, and he attempts to pull it over her head. "No, no!" Her voice is as weak as her struggle to hold to the gown. Why does she fight him? How can her modesty have any importance in such extremity of pain? Or does she fear him? Does she think he is trying to hurt her, or rape her? "Mom! It's me!"

He carries her to the bathroom. She feels terrifyingly light in his arms, like a Dachau victim too far gone to rescue. He balances her on the toilet seat while testing the water running into the tub against the tender skin of his wrist, that spot a razor so easily slices. When he has the tub half-filled, he lifts her in, kneeling to steady the bony slippery stick of her body. "No," she says, "no." He lathers a cloth and washes her slowly and very gently, cleansing the flaccid flesh of her thighs, the sparsely haired groin, and the long vertical scar, like a zipper in a flight jacket, where once was her left breast. Her remaining breast is a puckered sack. Her skin is the color of bone, mouth a toothless hole, upper lip darkened by sparse, coarse hair.

His father before his death had grown soft and hospital-flabby with a white pout of stomach and a pale, nearly hairless chest sagging in two milky bags.

In maneuvering her from the tub he gets as wet as he used to when bathing his daughter. She is shivering, so he pulls the last towel from the cabinet to blot dry her skin, then slips off the towel he is wearing and wraps her in it. Naked, he carries her down the hall.

His wife is standing in the doorway to his mother's room. She steps aside to let him pass by.

When he has his mother in a dry gown, he lays her in the hospital bed and covers her with a blanket. He glances at the door; his wife is gone. He wraps the towel back around his waist. The commode righted and carpet sponged, he gives his mother her medication, turns out the light and sits on a chair beside the bed. The room's dark is softened by a child's night-light in a baseboard socket. Gripping the cold bones of his mother's hand, he senses, as with an ear to a track one might hear an oncoming train, the cannibal cells grinding away inside her body. She works her gums, lips stitched by pain, as her eyes fix on something beyond him. He cannot recognize her now as the person through whose body he entered his life. She looks more like an old man or retarded child than she does the image he retains of his mother. He lightly kisses the sallow cheek, the temple, the dry lips. The wrinkles webbing her eyes slowly converge, and she sleeps.

The door is closed to the bedroom he shares with his wife. No light shows in the gap between door and frame.

Gutted by exhaustion, he goes into the living room. He drops onto the couch, pulling to his chin an afghan his mother crocheted when he was a boy, at a time when she and his father still saw their lives as opening onto possibilities.

Perhaps age in itself is a kind of wisdom. Eroding surface distinctions, it lays bare at last the basic identity beneath the decorative flourish of penis or breast. So the individual comes to be instructed in the simple, painful truth of what it means to be human. Age, perhaps, is the only wisdom.

His eyes snap open. A ghost stands over him. His wife wears a white nightgown. Cool fingertips touch his puffed lip.

"Come to bed."

He follows the ghost down the dark hall. Unable to find his pajamas, he slips naked into bed, shivering from cold. He dials his electric blanket to five.

And feels the rousing heat of his wife's bare back against his belly, her ridden-up gown a ridge against his chest. Joined, they rock slowly in the creaking bed. He would will this time to go on always, but in an abrupt burst of fire his backbone melts and is drawn down and shot out of him, the moment ecstatic, possessing both joy and pain, ending in release, and leaving him hunched slackly against the solid live warmth of the woman's body.

May his mother's death be a release this sweet; recognizing his thought as a prayer, he offers it for her sake to the spark lighting the heart of matter.

After a time his wife reaches back to press him more tightly to her. "Love?"

"Love," he answers.

Her breathing deepens and body goes limp. Above his head the digital clock flicks to 4:32.

His hand lightly touches the woman's hip, tracing and retracing the full curve, as though his fingers were determined to learn what secret flesh holds.

Berzerk

THE GAMES WE HAVE TO PLAY HERE

are Astro Blaster, Battlezone, Berzerk, Break Out, Crack Up, No Man's Land, Speed Demon, Torpedo, and War Wizard. There's three Pac Man and two Space Invader machines. Kids go crazy for them. We had pinballs but Tolles got rid of them. Pinball is dead, Tolles says.

Royce Tolles owns Electric Fantasies. He moans and groans about how much he has to shell out for the machines and pay me, but I know he is raking it in. He bought Alma gold earrings, real gold.

My game is Berzerk. First thing, there's these yellow robots out to zap you with their electric, they touch you. But they can't shoot. They're easy to wipe out. You just run your man at them and poke your fire button and you blow them to pieces. Like when Tolles shot this turkey buzzard. It was on a fence post. We were hauling back a new Crack Up in my truck and he says stop. He gets this leather bag he carries, it's like a purse, out from under the seat. He takes out a big shiny pistol. I say what's that for? You want to see a man can shoot, Clayton? He nailed that bird, there's nothing but a big puff of feathers. That's what you call a buzzard blizzard, Tolles says, and he laughs. In Berzerk, it's like that with the robots. You hit them, they go all

33

to pieces. But if you wipe out all the easy yellow ones right off, the machine throws the red shooting ones at you. So I just take one or two yellow ones first turn, like that's the best I can do, and the next turn only a couple more. Then I get a whole screen full of easy ones at fifty points each and I clear the board and get a bonus. That's the way to do it, you hope to rack up a big score.

ALMA BLESSINGS AND I HAVE BEEN LIVING TOGETHER

almost half a year now. Four months and three weeks. I can't complain. She has never once turned me down and I know I am a lucky man. I love her. First time I told her that she just laughed, cocking a hip the way she does, and said Love me? Shit! I make a great chili and I fuck like a mink. Count your blessings, Clayton.

I guess if she fools around it's her business. Like she says, she never said *I do* and wears no man's ring.

I OPEN UP ELECTRIC FANTASIES

at ten and there's always people waiting on me. Saturdays it's kids. During the week it's guys on their coffee break. Some of them joke about wasting their money when they hand you a bill, but most don't even notice you.

Tolles could put in a token machine but he's too cheap. I have to wear this apron, it jingles when I walk. He rents the games from some company. Mafia, he tells me, Cosa Nostra, buddy boy. Better watch our ass with the accounting, we don't want to end up in cement.

Tolles never lets me get my hands on the keys to the machines. All I can do is write up fake slips. How is the mafia going to know? Sometimes Tolles looks at the slips and says Damn, Clayton, these refunds are killing us. I keep my mouth shut. Then, like he does, he starts in laughing. I could laugh too, I am cheating him out of ten bucks a week, but I don't. I keep some things to myself.

ALMA WEARS SKINNY LITTLE UNDERPANTS

with *Muy Bueno* printed on the seat. She says it is Mexican for hot stuff. She's got a T-shirt says Hot and Cold right where her buttons are, like faucets.

I bought her a card for her birthday, in April, and it said

> *Darling, I love you*
> *Because you are special*
> *Because you are you*
> *Because I feel special*
> *When I am with you.*

It was on that shiny thick paper that feels like glass or waxed furniture. It had yellow roses on it. When she opened it her face got red. I hate this stupid fucking bullshit, Clayton! She slammed the door so hard going out my ears started in ringing.

I CAN'T SEE MYSELF AS A LEMON

eating up dots. Pac Man is a game for kids. In Space Invaders they're lined up like a shooting gallery, it's easy. It gets boring. Not Berzerk. Those robots are out to fry you. The walls will fry you too and so will the bouncing happy face, Evil Otto. You can't shoot Evil Otto or do anything but run away from him and he can go through walls and you can't. Even if you get out of the maze, it just gets harder the next time. The red robots shoot back. Get by them, there's white robots. They move real fast and they shoot like lightning. You're working your handle running your man around the maze and poking your fire button and the machine keeps going Intruder Alert, Intruder Alert! The Intruder Must Not Escape! and the white robots are coming at you zapping everything and here comes Evil Otto! You work up a sweat all right. And when you get to those purple ones! You're lucky to get off a shot before ZAP, BUZZ, that's all she wrote.

BECAUSE WE ARE NOT WORTHY,

Alma's mother told her, it isn't right to write His name. Let X stand for Christ. X-tianity, Alma writes it to show me. X-tians worship the big X.

Sex, Alma's mother said, is a woman's cross to bear.

I AM A FOOL TO GET STUCK HERE,

Tolles is always saying. Olentangy is a nowhere place. He is buying into this adult book store in Columbus, he says, but even so Ohio is a nowhere place. In the long run it's Florida for him, Key West. Or L.A. maybe.

Royce Tolles loves to play the big shot, silk shirts all colors and his gold chain and that big white Continental with its red leather seats. I don't let it get to me. In school he was nothing special, nothing more than me, I mean no brain or football player or nothing. We got out, his uncle got us work at the truck docks, out on Tractor Road. We were janitors. I did a lot better job than him. They said I was one of the best janitors they ever had. Tolles hardly did half his work. He was always running numbers and selling the drivers pills. That's what I wanted to be, a driver. Driving one of those big rigs and roaring on down the road all the way to Chicago or someplace. But it would be hard. I've banged up my pick-up just parking. It's rusted anyway. Tolles said I was stupid to want to drive a truck. No future in humping somebody else's load, he said. He quit his janitor job to sell cars. I bet his uncle was mad. Then he took off for Florida, couple years. Comes back, he's got his hair curled like a girl's, I almost don't know who he is. You want a job with a future, buddy boy? he wants to know. He tells me about this electric place he's opening up, how it's going to be a gold mine, bigger'n disco, and says, What do I want to do, push a broom the rest of my life? What about your uncle, I ask him. Screw him. Here, he says, and gives me a twenty dollar bill. That's your bonus, like athletes, you know. You signing on with me or not? I say okay. So here I am putting in sixty hours a week and what am I getting? Minimum wage, that's it. No more bonus business either. Alma says it's a crime.

BILLY JAY BUCK WAS IN VIETNAM AND COME BACK

with a medal. One night some of us are drinking beer on his back porch and he tells us about a real bad time when they got the shit shot out of them by Charlie and later they just up and shot the shit out of a bunch of old men and women and kids, to get even. He says the war really sucked. I say I wish I'd have been there. You stupid fuck! he screams. He is sitting right next to me and like to bust my ear. I jump off the porch and turn my ankle on a beer can and go down, banging my head. I bust my glasses right in half. I get up and damn if my nose isn't bleeding. There is blood on my clean T-shirt. I am so mad I could cry. Billy Jay Buck is standing up. You don't know shit, Clayton, he says. Nobody says anything. I pick up my glasses. I say, Well I know I don't have to stand around here taking any more of your shit. I walk out to my truck and tear hell out of his folks' gravel drive spinning out of there, one hand on the wheel and the other holding my glasses together.

Billy Jay Buck has got a chip on his shoulder because he didn't get a parade when he come home. So? I never got to go anyplace on account of my eyes. My job sucks too, but you don't catch me busting guys' glasses and making their nose bleed for them. Lots of people don't get parades.

ALMA USES TOOTHPASTE ON HER FACE

because she says that's the secret to clear skin. She does not have one pimple. Her face is as bright and clean as a little girl's. When she's not wearing any makeup. I wait till she gets done washing her face, then sneak in and kiss her. *Oh Clayton.* But she's not really mad. She smells clean and new, like peppermint.

But when she puts on makeup she makes her eyes so purple it looks like somebody has beat her up.

I AM A CAPITALIST, DOC TELLS ME, A TRUE ENTREPRENEUR

and I guess he knows. He's a teacher up at the college and he likes to come in here and play. When he's not drinking, he's not so bad. I told him about the business that Marty Freeman, who's utility man at Reliance Manhole and goes to the Freewill Baptist, is selling me. Marty says it is a steady income but what with his wife and kids he's looking to sell out. So I am taking it over, I tell Doc. I fill up the rubber machines in the men's rooms in eight bars, five gas stations, and two truck stops. I have to check them every week. But I don't tell Doc, I didn't even tell Alma, about paying off Marty Freeman with the money I am taking from Tolles. See, I tell Doc, I want to get something of my own. He says that's the lesson of American history. Only money makes money. Maybe someday you'll own your own company, Clayton's Condoms. Well, I don't know, I say. I show him the catalogue with all the different kinds you can get. We got regular, lubricated, reservoir tip, ridged, and scented, I tell him. I can get you Arouse, Contur, Fetherlite, Nuda, Ramses, Sheik, Touch, and Trojan. Holy Toledo, Doc says, I had no idea.

ALMA WAS A LATTER DAY SAINT

but isn't anything now. Great Grandpa Blessings in Provo had three wives. I got cousins all over the place out there, Alma says, like rabbits. Count your blessings, we were told, and we sure as hell had plenty to count. Only good a woman is to a Mormon is to make more Mormons. Nothing but a baby machine to them, Clayton. And a sinner. Oh do they love to forgive their sinners! Well, she says, I am finished with all that Tabernacle crap for the rest of my life, quit of it for good. And I'm glad, believe you me.

I think it's being brought up so religious that makes Alma not like me selling rubbers. I tell her Look right here on the package. This Product is Sold Only for the Prevention of Disease. Those things make me feel like *I'm* the disease, she says. How'd you like one of those little baggies stuck up your hole, Clayton?

When Alma gets mad she talks like that. She talks dirty when we make love too. And she twists her face up like she's in pain so I ask her, Do you want me to stop? and she says, Don't, Don't stop! I thought I was hurting you, I tell her when we're done, and she laughs. You always hurt me, Clayton. I say, Why is that? and she says, Because you are hung like a goddamned horse, that's why. Alma will say most anything. But I can't say I love her.

I wish I could wipe out all that Tabernacle crap and make her not feel hurt. When we're making love I pretend that's what I am doing, pushing it all out of her so she'll feel filled up with good. And be happy.

SAME OLD BULLSHIT, DOC SAYS,

when I ask him what is it like up at the college. He is playing No Man's Land, but isn't getting anywhere. This is the real world right here, he says.

I tell him Doc you know sometimes I feel like banging my head against a wall, I feel, I don't know, you know, like I'm just going to bang my head. It's the same with everybody, Doc says. Look at television, the movies. We live in crazy times, Clayton. Violence is our number one American sport. Or maybe number two, he says, and winks at me. Well, I say, maybe.

I SHOT ONE DEER THIS SEASON BUT IT WAS CERAMIC

only I thought it was real. Tolles let me go hunting with him and use his extra shotgun. He has shot lots of deer. I really wanted to get a deer before he did. Just to show him, you know, four-eyes and all, that I could do it. We didn't see anything but squirrels the whole day. Then we come out of the woods onto the road and I seen it. The light was poor and my glasses fogged up, but I whipped up that gun and took my shot. It was in a yard and a bald man come running out of the house yelling like crazy. I tore up that buck. It looked awful lifelike, the doe too. The bald man wanted to call the police but Tolles talked to him and told me to hand over two fives I had in my wallet and that was it.

Six point buck, Tolles says, and Dead Eye Clayton nails him smack in the ass! Everybody at the Ease On Inn is all ears. Alma is standing by the door to the kitchen. Tolles is laughing so hard he can hardly talk. A fucking lawn decoration! Everybody splits a gut. There's no point me trying to say anything. I keep my mouth shut. But it was near dark and that buck was a good thirty yards away.

ALMA LIKES CHICORY

and buys it ground up at the Safeway and puts it in our coffee. It makes it bitter the way she likes it.

One time we're taking a walk by the train tracks and Alma stops and says Oh Clayton, look! There is Chicory and Queen Anne's Lace mixed in together, blue and white, white and blue. She says it looks like a quilt her grandma in Utah made for her. Alma used to cover up with that quilt when she was little and look out her window and wonder how far up the sky went. She starts crying when she tells me that. I want to be *her* again, Clayton! I kiss her and she grabs hold of me like I am the most special thing in the world.

WHAT ARE WE RUNNING HERE, AN ORPHANAGE?

Tolles yells at me. He runs off the kids hanging around cause they don't know where else to go. Pay to play or make tracks, that's what you tell them. What do you think I am, a social worker? And don't give me that look, buddy boy. I'm telling you something here for your own good. Let people walk on you, they'll do it. Gladly. Come back tomorrow, do it again. How the hell you think I got this place? My car, my apartment? Hustle, buddy boy, hustle. I see my chance, I take it. Better nobody get in my way either. Less they wanna end up on crutches. Jesus Christ, you getting *any* of this? Clayton?

TOLLES AND ALMA ARE FOOLING AROUND

but I can't say anything. He can take her out to fancy places, dancing and all. She wants some fun out of life, I know. Still and all, I could kick myself black and blue for ever taking Alma to work with me. I just had to show Mr. Big Shot what a pretty girl I got. I know what goes on between them. Sometimes it pops into my head and I want to knock it loose. But it goes away.

OUR BABY COULD WATCH THE ANIMALS GO AT IT

and know it was natural and fun, Alma says. If we had a place in the country. If we ever wanted to have a baby. We are in bed and she is smoking dope. Clayton, she says, we could have chickens and cows. Maybe a horse. We could have a small house and a big garden. You got shoulders big enough I could hitch you to a plow. You'd make a good farmer. A good Daddy too.

But we wouldn't ever hit our baby and call him stupid, I tell Alma. And we wouldn't ever go away and leave him alone all night. No, we'd never do that, Alma says. Our baby would be beautiful like me, and good-hearted like you. You're good-hearted, I tell her. No, Alma says, you, you've got a big heart. That's what I like about you. Then she laughs the way she does. That and this other big thing.

YOU WANT TO GO ONE ON ONE, BERZERK?

I ask Billy Jay Buck when he comes in. He looks around, shaking his head. What *is* this shit? You got kids playing Search and Destroy, Nuclear Holocaust, what? You want to play or not? I ask him. So we drop our tokens and I rack up 19,860 points to his 1,210. He acts like it's no big thing. I tell him I am surprised he come back from Vietnam, he's such a bad shot. He looks like he's about to bust my glasses again, which I got taped together so they'll stay on my face. Tolles keeps a shotgun behind the counter, a twelve gauge. I would have the law on my side if I got it out and gave Billy Jay Buck a good scare. But he don't do anything, he just goes.

YOU KILL ME, CLAYTON, YOU REALLY DO,

Alma says. Little things I do. Like I will only wear white socks cause they won't give you a foot infection you get a blister. And play a harmonica though I don't know any real songs, only train sounds. And when Alma's tips at the Ease On Inn are poor, I just hand her my wallet and say, Help Yourself. You really do, she says.

Sometimes we sit up late and I have a beer and she smokes some dope she brings home. I know she gets it from Tolles, maybe he gets it from the Mafia, but I don't say anything. She gets silly and starts in tickling me and we roll around on the rug. I like this time the best of all. It's like we are brother and sister. Alma's eyes are real clear and deep brown. They look like a deer's eyes. We wrestle around and I let her hold me down like she is stronger. Then she grabs me right by my handle and sticks me in her like I was a knife. I get scared when she acts like this, but I don't tell her.

CONGRATULATIONS, YOU HAVE JOINED
THE IMMORTAL RANKS

of top scorers. You may now enter your initials. That is what the screen tells you when you rack up a bigger score than anybody else up there that day. I have got so good at Berzerk I can get all the top slots.

1.	COG	18,430
2.	COG	16,260
3.	COG	15,010
4.	COG	14,800
5.	COG	13,430
6.	COG	13,260
7.	COG	13,200
8.	COG	13,180
9.	COG	11,860
10.	COG	10,720

That stands for Clayton Otis Gabriel, I tell people. That's me. Doc says it's amazing. He can barely get 5,000. I guess I am the best there is at this game, I say.

Tolles doesn't want me putting my name up there. It takes the fun out of it for the customers. So I don't do it anymore. Just once in a while. Some of the punks that come in here think it's fun to put up things like FUK, TIT, DIK. They do that, I come over and rack up a big score and put me up there instead. That's okay with Tolles. He says he wants this to be a family place. Punks don't have any money.

When Alma is coming, I rack up all the top scores. Punks were in, I tell Tolles. I show Alma. Clayton, she says, you are really something. She laughs and Tolles laughs, so I do too.

ALMA WANTS TO OWN A HOUSE AND NOT GET OLD
and sit around worried sick about the rent and if her social
security is coming or not. She says that all Bessie, the old waitress
at the Ease On Inn, ever talks about is her worries and complaints. Oh my God, the taxes! Oh my God, the arthritis! I ever
get that bad, Alma says, I will sit myself down in a tub of warm
water with a quart of vodka and a fistful of red devils. Nytol!

Alma hates paying rent. She lays awake nights thinking about
the rent coming due and our mattress not being paid for yet and
how she's still paying off her charge for clothes she got which
are already gone out of style. *I* feel rented, Alma says. I hate that
feeling. It's like I don't own myself. At work I feel like just
another old chair or table. I get worn out, they just toss me out.
I can't stand to think of working like this—for nothing, for
other people. Not for the rest of my natural born life, Clayton.
I just can't.

I tell her now that I got a start in a business of my own, things
will get better. Alma says, Oh Clayton, please! You're never
going to have anything but that stupid old truck. I'm going to
get it dinged out, I say, maybe sandblasted and painted. No,
you're just too good-hearted, Clayton. Good-hearted people stay
poor, that's all there is to it. But I am saving up my money, I
tell her. You think Tolles is so smart, but maybe I know a trick
or two. That's what gets me, Alma says. Royce won't do an
honest day's work. All he does is use people to make more
money. It makes me sick. I thought you liked him, I say. I hate
him, Alma says, I hate his guts.

I hold her in the dark. I am glad that she hates Tolles. I was
scared she was falling in love with him.

GOD MAKES US SUFFER DOWN HERE
TO READY US FOR ETERNAL LIFE,
Alma's mother told her. Else, we would be no better than
animals wanting nothing more than to live on earth forever.
This way, death comes as a blessing.

ALMA AND TOLLES LOOK LIKE STARS

in a movie or on TV. I have just closed up and have 17,600 points going in Berzerk when they come in. They are all dressed up. Tolles bought Alma this long gold dress she is wearing. He's got on tooled cowboy boots and a white silk shirt, and that gold chain around his neck. He stands by the door, puffing on a cigarillo. He's got his leather bag hanging from his shoulder. He thinks he's something. Alma is giggly. I know she has been smoking dope. Smoking dope helps her to forget things, she says. I guess it helps her forget how much she hates Royce Tolles' guts. They are going to a club that needs dancers, Alma tells me. Royce's friend owns it. Do you think I'll be a good exotic dancer, Clayton? I guess so, I say. You *guess* so? Alma says. I got a dynamite body, I got all the moves, and you guess so? She starts dancing around, that gold dress like electric lights. Tolles asks could they please get a move on, it's getting late. Clayton, Alma says, I am going to make some real money. If that's what you want to do, I say. *If* I want to? Alma makes big eyes at me. What, I'm stupid or something?

I don't like Alma acting like this. I think maybe she has been drinking too. I know it hurts her when she acts mean. Lots of times I have held her when she was crying about some mean thing she did or said, crying until her nose ran and got red and her eyes puffed up. If Tolles saw her looking like that I bet he'd be surprised.

You're that stupid, Clayton, Alma says, but not me. You want to know how stupid Clayton is? she asks Tolles. Baby, he says, I know, I know. No you don't, she says. Clayton is so stupid he thinks he loves me. You ever hear of anything that stupid? Royce? Hey, Tolles says, we going somewhere or not? I only wanted to stop by and see good old Clayton, Alma says. She gives me a peck on the cheek. Wish me luck, Clayton? She sticks a hand in my apron and jingles my tokens. I guess so, I say. I told you not to love me, Alma says. I can't help it, I tell her, I do. Jesus, Tolles says, I can't believe this bullshit. He throws his cigarillo on the floor I have to sweep up and grabs

Alma's arm. Hey, I tell him, if she don't want to go with you, you know, she don't have to. Buddy boy, Tolles says, please do not stick your nose in where it does not belong. He pulls on Alma and she almost falls down. I grab hold her other arm. She hates you, I tell him, she hates your guts. He slaps me. My glasses fly apart and my cheek stings like crazy. I knock him down. He unzips his bag and Alma grabs it away from him. He jumps up. You bitch! he says. Don't call her that, I tell him. He is pulling on the strap but Alma won't let go. I go behind the counter. Tolles yells Gabriel you stupid sonuvabitch you pick that fucker up and you're fired. I pick up the shotgun. It's the one I shot the deer with. That tears it, he says, get your ass outta my place.

Alma stands there with her arms wrapped tight around the bag, holding it to her chest. She is crying, shaking her head. Oh Clayton, I'm sorry. I am no good, no damned good. I mess up everything.

I pump the gun.

You hear me, Tolles yells, I mean *fast*!

ALL I HAVE TO DO IS PULL THE TRIGGER,

I tell him, I can't miss. You won't bother her anymore ever. Just like you see on TV. Blow you all to pieces.

Clayton, Alma says, don't. They'll lock you up, Tolles says. He moves like he's trying to hide behind Alma but I say stop and he does. That what you want, Clayton? They'll lock you up in a box, you'll never see the light of day. Don't, Clayton, Alma says. He's not worth it. Then they walk out.

EVERYBODY KNOWS ABOUT IT BY THE TIME
I WAKE UP

and they all want to know what do I think. Give me a chance, I say. I hear it on the radio all day and then I read it in the paper. I am just sick. It's Tolles' fault, that's what I tell anybody asks me. You can bet on that. He was always trouble, nothing but. You know Alma. She's good-hearted. She would never hurt anybody, she didn't have to.

I LOOK EVERYWHERE FOR ALMA

but people say she's in Columbus, a hotel. I'm glad she's not in jail. Bessie says Mr. Moore is her lawyer and I go ask him. He's a fat man. I can't see her until the court, he says. He wants me there, too. I'm important.

THE KNIFE LOOKS LIKE ANY KITCHEN KNIFE

like you'd slice onions with or potatoes. There's a white tag on it. It's on a table at the front of the room. Royce Tolles' pistol is up there too. There's a flag on a pole. We have to stand when the judge comes in. He has white hair.

Alma looks awful. She is wearing a nice blue dress I never saw. Her eyes are purple and black but it's not makeup. It hurts me to look at her. She looks like she has been crying for weeks.

And I don't like to look at the knife. I keep seeing it sticking in Tolles.

When Alma sits in the chair up front she sits up real straight. She won't look at me. Maybe she's mad. I don't want her locked up in a box. I should've done it, but I couldn't, I don't know why. I never killed anything. This man asks her and she says she is not a whore and never has been one. I can see how mad she is. I keep waiting for her to tell him she can't stand this stupid bullshit but she doesn't. She's crying. He keeps asking and asking. He asks her about me too. People look at me when he says my name. I look right at Alma. I am harmless, that's what she says, I have nothing to do with it. He asks her one thing after another. I don't like him. He acts like he doesn't believe her at all.

Another day I have to go up there and they put my hand on the Bible. I promise to tell the truth. I do. Mr. Moore asks me and I tell them about the Mormons and how Alma is real religious. And about Tolles working for the Mafia. How he shot that bird. Alma hated his guts, I say, I did too. Mr. Moore says that's enough, thank you. But I say we are sorry about him anyway.

The other one wants to know about my rubber machines and

how did Alma make her money. He's got curly hair like Tolles. I say Alma was a real hard worker. And they can ask Marty Freeman, I tell him, the machines are still his.

SELF-DEFENSE IS A PERSON'S RIGHT

Mr. Moore says. He walks around and talks loud, like he is mad at them all. Even in his apartment. Tolles hit her, the neighbors heard him, they heard her begging him to stop. Now I ask you, he says, would you have her wait until he got his gun?

When they say Alma won't have to go to jail, I am so happy! Alma is too. She kisses Mr. Moore right there in front of everybody. I buy her daisies, a big bunch. It costs a dollar-fifty to have them delivered.

FINALLY ALMA COMES BACK TO OUR PLACE

but she says only to pick up her things. I want you here, I tell her. No, she says, she has to get out of here. She hates Olentangy. Well, I got nothing to tie me down, I say, where you want to go? She starts crying. She has to be by herself, she says. I hold her and won't let go and then we are kissing and kissing, we just can't stop. I pick her up and carry her to our mattress. Clayton, Alma says, Oh Clayton! I know she won't ever go away.

I GO TO BED IN THE MORNING NOW

and get up when it's dark. It is so cold out, snow and ice all over. I cook my supper. It's my breakfast, I guess. Then I pack my lunch. I eat that at three o'clock in the morning.

Bargain Barn is scary at night, it is so big and makes creaky noises. I am alone in here. They gave me a pistol to carry, it's an American Bulldog. I bring my harmonica and a thermos of coffee with my lunch. The shirt and pants they gave me are blue.

I ALWAYS READ THE COMICS AND DEATH NOTICES

when I get the paper. I like Buz Sawyer and Terry and the Pirates. Sometimes you read where somebody kills himself.

Most of the time they don't even leave a note to tell why. Sometimes I put the American Bulldog up to my head to see how it feels, but I don't ever do anything. It feels cold.

I GOT A BIG POSTCARD WITH A BABY DEER ON IT

from Alma, in Maine. I am a good person and she will never forget me. You have to learn to believe in yourself, Clayton. She hopes I am taking care of myself. Did I get my truck painted? She feels awful about what happened. When she feels really bad though, she remembers they said *not* guilty. Guess what? She's taking a course at the community college, psychology. It's really interesting. Her teacher knows everything, and he is so young. He says she's not stupid at all. The Lobster Trap, where she's working, is okay. Still, she is looking for something better.

WHEN I AM ALL DONE

sweeping I use a TV to play video games. They have Asteroids, Hangman, Maze Craze, Missile Command, Night Driver, and Warlords. I have got pretty good at Missile Command. It's hard. The missiles are coming down on you all different ways. You have to spin this ball to get your X on a target, then push a button to shoot your missiles. You have to go like crazy, both hands. When all your cities get wiped out, there's this big orange flash and a white cloud and then it says THE END.

Teller's Ticket

The basic purpose of the ticket arrangement was to minimize if not completely eliminate difficulties, certainly not to cause more, and not by any stretch of the imagination to land Teller in such a hapless predicament that he wished he'd never conceived of the system.

He drove his white Rabbit at the legal limit in the expressway's slushy right lane, the gray wake of a tractor-trailer enveloping him as in a cloud. His windshield wipers slapped back and forth at a manic rate yet failed to clear his field of vision. The rear of the semi, intermittently visible, bore a yellow sticker with black block lettering: MY LIGHTS ARE ON FOR SAFETY. Teller's lights were on high. He wore his shoulder harness and seat belt. He felt utterly unsafe.

Teller believed on principle in conducting one's life in an orderly manner. Had his life worked out according to plan— he'd had his heart set on being elected a U.S. senator—he would have applied his idea of order to the affairs of the nation. He had failed to win election, however, to either city council or the local school board. Adjusting downward his career aims, he now labored as a lobbyist for Hartford Health Insurance. The statehouse was his beat. Bills affecting health care plans bore his anonymous stamp, and tens of thousands of heartland citizens were unknowingly in his debt for their extended coverage. Teller took satisfaction in pulling strings behind the scenes.

Nina, his wife, was a coronary care nurse. The Tellers' common interest was health. They jogged, dieted, and did slimnastics together. They drank only in moderation. Neither smoked. Had they chosen to have children, their offspring never would have become those lank and languid social excesses one saw smoking grass in city parks or lining up at public clinics for the legalized manna of methadone.

Not that Teller and Nina had no problems. Any two people living together for any length of time, whether husband and wife, parent and child, sibling and sibling, or POSSLQ's (persons of the opposite sex sharing living quarters, as per U.S. census category), had problems. Teller, as he did in influencing bills and amendments, applied his considerable talents for meticulous analysis and reasoned compromise to his marital difficulties.

So how in the world had he gotten himself into this idiotic imbroglio—that's what he'd like to know.

Once a week he played poker, his minor vice. His doctor, Art Easterday, hosted the games at his comfortably cluttered bachelor's quarters. There was usually another doctor or two in attendance, besides Bill Modell, a pipe-sucking ad exec addicted to high stakes bluffing, and a CPA named Veering who was Teller's only match in estimating the odds of a given hand. Teller, although he infrequently won big, rarely ended up a loser. He folded early on weak cards, stood pat on a fair draw, seldom bluffed, and when blessed with a winning hand sucked in bets with artful raises.

Last night he had suffered a three-hour run of bad cards before being dealt, at midnight, four kings in a round of draw. He discarded a deuce, and drew an ace of spades. He bumped a raise and a bifocaled gynecologist folded. Easterday, an excessive mound of chips before his expansive paunch, met and raised Teller. Veering closed his eyes for a moment, consulting his internal calculator, before tossing in his hand. Modell called. Teller raised. Easterday raised again, giving Teller pause. Easterday too had drawn a single card, which probably meant he was drawing to a straight or a flush (the doctor's weakness was for filling inside straights) or was also holding four of a kind. Even so, Easterday couldn't do better than queens. Moving to raise, Teller noted with dismay that his run of bad luck had left him bereft of chips. It was the biggest pot of the entire night.

"You out?" Modell prompted, chomping at the bit to sweeten the pot. It appeared that the only reason he played was to prove how much he could afford to lose.

Teller produced his wallet. He had filled up his Rabbit's tank and had gotten his hair trimmed; two crinkled ones were all he had left. His checkbook was at home. Easterday displayed on his boneless face the mild smile that never failed to infuriate Teller. He fished out his one remaining monthly ticket, tapped its stiff edge on the table a moment, considering. Then, promising himself that he'd make up to Nina for his indiscretion with a gala evening out on his winnings, he placed the ticket atop the loaded pot.

Had he felt in his bones at that moment that he teetered on the brink of a deadly precipice? Now, he could not be certain. Then, he knew only that the pot was his.

Easterday picked up the ticket, read it, raised his eyebrows, and laid it back down. "I don't think you want to do this."

"Hey, what's going on here?" Modell was aiming the ticket at Teller's head.

The ticket was Teller's prize: *This entitles the bearer to one sex act of his choice.* Nina's signature slanted across the lower part of the card.

"I assume you can read," Teller said to Modell, then to the banker: "That ought to be worth at least fifty."

"I'd say a hundred at the very least," Easterday replied.

"A hundred it is," Teller snapped, a generous grin covering his pique at being topped by the doctor. "After all, it's your money." He resolutely appeared calm as the others looked first at the ticket and then at him with what he took to be a new regard.

Modell complained, "I thought this was table stakes."

"Pot limit," Teller reminded him.

Easterday leaned forward as he did in professional consultation. "I believe you are making a serious mistake."

"The question is, are you a gambler or not?" Teller let that sink in, then fixed Modell with a penetrating stare. "Too rich for your blood, big boy?"

"What the hell!" Modell flipped in ten blue chips.

"You're being foolish," Easterday said.

"Hey, it's my money," Modell whined.

"I was speaking to Byron."

If Teller had considered backing down and treating the incident as his little joke, Easterday's patronizing tone stiffened his resolution. Why did doctors think the world was obligated to defer to them? A man too old for his years, who obviously needed to be put on a strict diet, Easterday was forever giving Teller advice: slow down, develop a hobby, take your poor wife on vacation. When Teller countered that he knew how to manage his affairs, the doctor would only smile. Easterday seemed determined not to treat Teller as an equal. Had Teller risen to the Senate, he'd have sponsored a socialized medicine bill to put Easterday and his ilk in their place. "Does that mean you fold?" Teller asked.

Easterday blue-chipped the pot.

"Showdown!" Modell trumpeted, slapping down his pathetic full house. Easterday held a straight flush, hearts, queen high. Teller splayed his losing kings. He sensed the others' close attention. "Win some, lose some," he said. Rising from his chair, he donned his parka and went out to his Rabbit, the heart in his chest as frantic as a snared bird.

Now, his hands clutched the steering wheel like a lifeline. His nerves sang with the stored tension of a sleepless night and a distracted day at work. How to tell Nina what he had done? For after his noon confrontation with Easterday it was apparent that an explanation of sorts would be necessary. It wasn't only that he'd lost the ticket, but that he had dared show it to anyone. Nina would leave him, or kill him. She had always been the less rational partner in their marriage.

Although, to give her her due, she had come to admit the practicality of the ticket arrangement. The Tellers' bone of contention was sex, as it appeared to be with the majority of married couples, and he'd seen no reason that the problem could not be dealt with in a rational manner. Not given to hot-tubbing, standing on his head while chanting a mantra, nor self-hypnotizing his system into proper biorhythms, Teller sought release from tension in sex. Since he was on principle monogamous, Nina necessarily provided any release beyond that which he might handle himself. Teller's sexual needs were daily, Nina's weekly. Such disparity might drive some couples into divorce court to sunder their union and fragment their estate. None of that avoidable messiness for Teller. A booklet of detachable, redeemable love coupons spotted in a novelty shop prompted his plan. In consultation with his wife, he composed a series of fifteen monthly tickets on the reverse side of his business cards, fourteen tickets specifying particular sexual acts and a special one giving him free choice. Nina was issued three counter-claims to allow for occasional indisposition. Despite his wife's initial discomfiture, Teller felt reasonably assured that his system was both equitable and viable. Having read Kinsey, Masters and Johnson, *The Joy of Sex, More Joy*, Nancy Friday and Gay Talese, he was quite cognizant of the fact that the sexual revolution had rendered obsolete traditional strictures and customs. There was a whole lot of coupling going on, and Teller saw no reason that a loyal spouse need miss out on the action, not when he was capable of plotting a course of corrective action.

Of course Nina felt somewhat differently about it. Her lovemaking, although more regular since the system's inception, was marked by a sense of distance. Teller fully expected, however, that it would take time for her to adjust to such a frank and open

approach to matters she'd been taught to regard as dark, dangerous secrets. Nina had been raised in the Roman Catholic religion,
that primitive cult designed to scar one deeply enough in child-
hood that the remainder of one's life would be devoted to rituals
in hope of a miraculous cure. Teller's parents were Christian
Scientists. Although he practiced no religion, Teller did not in-
veigh against others' beliefs. While it was true that when travel-
ing he relieved his motel room of the Gideon Bible, disposing of
it in the nearest trash can, it had nothing to do with religion. He
resisted on principle the invasion of one's privacy.

Which was precisely the reason he resented Easterday so. The
good doctor was invading the Tellers' privacy now by pressing
his claim just as surely as if he were inserting a rubber-gloved
finger into Teller's rectum, which he did every six months. As
he also did to Nina.

Could it be that having taken Pap smears, palpated her breasts,
rapped her dimpled knees with his rubber-headed hammer,
peered down her throat, lit up her ear canals and pupils, and
listened to her heart beat, that Easterday secretly lusted for Nina?

In a moment of giddy paranoia Teller imagined the fat
physician as having run the poker game for years waiting as
patiently as a bullfrog for the butterfly of opportunity that last
night had provided. Not so paranoid perhaps. Hadn't Teller
off-handedly mentioned his ticket system during his recent
physical? Hadn't Easterday displayed definite interest, his eyebrows lifting, and a light coming on in his eyes which Teller
saw now as one not of surprise but rather of excitement? Not
paranoia at all. The proof, if indeed Teller needed any, had come
that noon when he'd tried to buy back his ticket. "I'm afraid
that's not possible," Easterday had said. Teller had expected him
to hand it over with a chuckle, to treat the affair as a joke between friends, a pardonable bit of gaucherie which Teller would
pay for with rueful smiles and patient endurance of the doctor's
waggish jibes. Teller doubled, then tripled, his offer. "What's lost
is lost," was Easterday's reply.

"What kind of man are you anyway?" Teller had shrieked.

"The question is—" A slow grin suffused Easterday's pallid face, "—are you a gambler or not?"

Teller had slammed the door in leaving, nearly bowling over the young office nurse whom the fat quack no doubt spread-eagled on his desk after hours. Easterday probably had possessed dozens of women, no doubt illicitly diddling scores of his patients. What did he care if he shattered marriages, ruined people's lives, made it impossible for a man ever again to look his wife straight in the eye?

Nina's tan Rabbit was in the drive. Teller whipped in behind her. He entered their paid-for split-level as anxiously as a fire-fighter a blazing tenement.

"Any calls?" he called, his usual greeting sounding ominous to him. What did Easterday say? What did you say? What can I say to make it okay?

"Nothing," Nina called from the bathroom. She always popped into the tub directly on arriving home; it was hard work nursing hearts back to health.

Teller made a cup of Sanka and sagged into his armchair. Slowly, now that he was home and enclosed by known walls, some sense of safety returned.

Of course there existed not the slightest possibility that Nina would honor Easterday's ill-gotten claim. Medical ethics, marriage vows, and moral concerns gave her the perfect right to turn him away empty-handed. Moreover, strictly on a technical level, she had left one monthly counter-claim. The Tellers would scout about for a new doctor and that would be the end of the affair. Teller could explain to his wife that he'd had too much to drink that night, implying perhaps that his host may have spiked his drink. The fact that he rarely drank would only serve as further reason for his unaccountably erratic behavior.

Why was he thinking defensively? The situation called for action. Teller would sit his wife down and frankly explain to her that he had cause for concern. It appeared that one of his tickets had turned up missing. To make no bones about it, he'd lost it. They needed to be prepared for the unlikely event that someone might find it and, misunderstanding the nature of the Tellers' intimate agreement, attempt to redeem it.

Easterday had witnesses, though. Still, Teller found it difficult to believe the doctor would have the gall to call on them. And if he did? Why then he was lying and the others were lying too. At bottom, who was Nina going to believe—a bunch of drunken gambling braggarts, or her own husband?

Secure in his wife's trust, Teller felt his heart expand in magnanimity. To clear the air he would propose they drop the ticket system altogether. "I know you're not nuts about it, kid, so what say we forget it?" Well, not *kid*. He'd broach the subject as soon as she completed her bath, then take her out to dinner, someplace swank, and afterwards they might go dancing if she liked, or to a movie, or shopping, whatever. Actually though, he might better wait until they came home, buoyant with fun and champagne-giggly, before mentioning the ticket's loss in an offhand manner, a comical happenstance to amuse the two of them in years to come as they looked back from the snug comfort of maturity at their feckless youth.

The telephone rang. Teller froze.

"Would you get that?" Nina called.

Teller plucked up the receiver and replaced it on its cradle. "Wrong number," he shouted. He waited beside the phone. Pouncing, he strangled the first ring before it fully sounded, then left the phone off the hook.

He ran upstairs for his checkbook, changed his shirt and tie, and rapped on the bathroom door. "Shake a leg, sweetheart. I'm treating you to dinner."

Nina opened the door. Her small body encased in a nubby white towel, a turban of white hiding her hazel hair, she looked heartbreakingly innocent. Teller's glasses misted with steam. He saw her as a fetching waif he'd seduced only to sell into white slavery. Never could he tell her what he'd done, no matter how much champagne they'd had.

She smiled up at him. "What's the occasion?"

Assaulted by an image of Easterday as a giant pulsating larval creature bearing down on Nina, Teller blurted "You look lovely!"

"Why, thank you."

Urgent signals of disconnection sounded. "I'll get it!" Teller bounded downstairs to suffocate the phone with couch cushions.

Only one course of action lay open to him. Easterday's lust could not be so great that he was willing to die for it.

When they returned home from dinner and a movie, Nina dressed for bed. Teller sat staring at premium redemption forms at his study desk.

"Aren't you coming?" She was wearing her plum, empire-style nightgown, his favorite, and his heart stuttered as his eyes took them in, her gold hoop earrings and slave bracelet.

"Some business." Feeling her soft breasts against the back of his head, he resisted an urge to rise.

An hour later he tiptoed to the open door of their bedroom. She was sleeping. He eased downstairs to the phone. On the sixth ring, the toad's voice croaked "Hello?"

A handkerchief over the mouthpiece, Teller rasped "Better listen and listen good, fat man. You're in a jam, understand. You're in way over your head."

"Byron, whom do you think you are fooling?"

"I ain't saying who hired me. But I'm warning you, Sawbones, I get a contract, I get it done. I don't mess and I don't miss. You get on my list . . ."

The doctor clicked off. Teller wiped perspiration from his face with the handkerchief, then carefully replaced the weapon in its holder.

Addressing the mystery voice as Byron was more than a shot in the dark, of course, but Easterday could not be one hundred percent certain who the caller was. He had to be suffering some apprehension, if not terror.

Teller would confront Easterday first thing in the morning. Lay it on the line. "Five hundred cash. It's an offer you can't refuse."

The telephone rang. Teller seized the receiver, holding it six inches from his ear and watching it from the corner of an eye, the cord snaking about his wrist.

"Did you lose something?" The doctor's voice was saturated with the oil of self-satisfaction.

Teller's hand sagged to the cradle. How could a sensitive, sensible human being do this to a fellow creature? Easterday was often a joyous dinner guest at Teller's laden table. He'd sung the praises of Nina's cooking, of Nina's decorating, of Nina's nursing. How could he treat her like a common whore?

Teller's body trembled. He was furious, he thought; outraged. He didn't have to stand for such abuse. He knew people in power, he had connections on the state medical board, he was skilled in legal ins and outs. A supposedly reputable physician making late night crank calls to his patients! He'd have Easterday's license revoked. He'd haul the fat man into court on harassment charges. Tack on alienation of affections too. Any attorney worth his salt . . .

Teller hugged himself. He was terrified.

The next three days were hell for Teller. He calculated his moves about the house always to be nearer than Nina to the phone. He ate little and became the victim of aspirin-immune headaches. Sleeping fitfully, listening for the telephone or doorbell or a car turning into their drive, he felt acid bubbling in his stomach. When Nina touched him in bed, he turned his back to her, pleading fatigue.

Each day he left his office early to be home when Nina arrived. "Anything interesting happen today? Anything new?"

"Is there something wrong?" she asked.

"Work," he explained.

He knew he was beaten. The lost ticket had become a San Andreas fault underlying the seven year construction of their marriage. The claim presented would shift the earth, bringing who knew what all down about their ears.

And might the earth move for Nina with Easterday? As it had

for Maria in *For Whom the Bell Tolls*? As it did less and less frequently for Nina with Teller?

Why had he done such a crazy thing? He'd known deep down that it was more than a joke. Yet in spite of his trembling hands, he'd gambled the ticket like a man on easy terms with deviance and danger. In fact, he saw now, placing the ticket on the gaming table was every bit as dangerous as if he'd plunked down a loaded revolver. It provoked unavoidable consequences. But surely he hadn't thought so at the time. At the time he'd thought of nothing but securing the loaded pot. His bet was a sure thing, damn it! No one needed to take the ticket seriously. It was only there for show. Until Easterday's fluke of luck ruined everything.

Yet hadn't Teller at times sensed that the tickets, while apparently no more than convenient possessions, were charged with a possibly destructive power? Like money or cars or firearms?

If he'd suffered such doubts, they were easily dismissed by the flush feelings of sufficiency and control he had felt as his well-being. Ticketed Teller was a man to behold, there was confidence in his stride and steel in his eye; no-ticket Teller was a bum on his uppers, scrounging gutters for stogie stubs.

The truth was inescapable. He was a fool.

But Easterday! He was worse than a fool. An unprincipled opportunist, he would press his advantage although it caused crisis and anguish for people who had thought of him as healer and friend. What could the hypocritical physician, brain in his groin, hope to comprehend of the Tellers' complex human union? Teller and Nina shared so many memories, understood one another's codewords and looks, made allowances for moods and quirks, counterbalanced particular weaknesses with particular strengths. Teller needed Nina. She was like a best friend to him. Struck by the possibility of losing her, Teller saw that she *was* his best friend. The doctor, of course, saw her as another usable body. Why hadn't Teller recognized this weakness earlier?

The next day he left work at noon, legitimately claiming a migraine, and lunched on Excedrin and Tums. He knew he had to tell her, and the sooner the better. He went shopping. At Fredericks of Hollywood he bought Nina a black silk affair split to the hip on either side. Minutes later he returned it. At Sears he got the fuzzy green sleepsack he knew she'd prefer. He ran from the shopping mall to his parked car, sleet needling his cheeks.

Home, he rooted about in Nina's things. He found the pack of redeemed tickets bound by a rubber band and tucked in a drawer beneath his wife's white panties. Building a fire on the hearth, he tossed the tickets into the blaze. When they were reduced to ash, he wrapped the sleepsack in gold foil and stuck a green silk bow on the package, then sat in his armchair, allowing himself a snifter of sherry for courage. Three-thirty came and went. He phoned the hospital and found that Nina had left there at three.

The calendar magnet-stuck to the refrigerator gave him the reason: 3:30, Doctor. So the meeting had been arranged. Easterday must have gotten to her at work. There was nothing for Teller to do but take his lumps.

He was working on a second snifter—consolation now—when he jerked to attention. A knot popped in the grate. *His* lumps? Nina was the one being lumped with those personless, glossy bodies laid bare in centerfolds, stylish latrines for men's ease.

He sped off in his Rabbit. The sleet turned to snow on his windshield.

Nina sat in the waiting room reading *Family Circle.* Her face registered alarm when she saw him. "What are you doing here?"

The office nurse slid back a glass slat. "Mrs. Teller, the doctor will see you now."

"That's what he thinks!" Teller threw open the door and barged down the hall. Behind him he heard Nina call his name.

"Aha!" Easterday cried. "The high-roller! Or is this the pimp? Or the hit man?"

"Let's have it, Fatso."

"Have what?"

"My ticket!" Teller roared.

The door opened and Nina looked in. "Your what?"

Easterday exploded with an enormous laugh. "Your ticker is fine!" He grasped Teller by the arm, there was great strength in his oleaginous hand, and placed him in a plastic chair. "This husband of yours!" he said to Nina. "At poker the other night I told him he had a weak heart. I'm afraid he misunderstood me. Nina, dear, would you mind waiting a few more minutes?" He winked. "Man talk." He edged her into the hall and closed the door.

"I'm not leaving here without it," Teller cried, springing to his feet. "If you lay a hand on her, it'll be over my dead body."

"So what is your offer now?"

"Whatever you want."

"Anything?"

"Name it."

Easterday creased his massive rump on the edge of his costly desk. "Surely you wouldn't go so far as to offer to take your wife's place?"

"What?"

"To redeem the ticket, you would take her place?"

Dizzied, Teller slumped into the chair.

"Well, Byron?"

He saw the doctor's smile as a sign of degenerate delight. The consulting room became a sultan's chamber. He detected in the air a hint of jasmine: Easterday's cologne? A confirmed bachelor —what a farce! The truth was only too clear to Teller now. He slammed a door in his mind against a rush of disgusting images. An act done out of love was above disgust. He would do it out of love for Nina. Whatever the doctor desired could be no worse than what Teller had demanded she do for him. "Anything," he managed to say.

"As a gambling man, you understand, it does interest me to know whether or not you are bluffing."

Teller met and held the doctor's gelid stare. "You want to find out, you've got to call."

Easterday sighed, a flatulent elephant. "Your ticket was thrown away right after our game."

63

"What?"

"It has gone the way of all trash."

"Why didn't you tell me?"

"Did you ask?"

"I offered . . ."

"You actually believed I could bring myself to mention a thing like that? To Nina, of all people?"

"Then why didn't you just give it back to me?"

"And have you use it?"

A flare went off in the dark of Teller's skull. When jogging had given him knee pains, he'd joked about having prosthetic joints put in that would work better than the original equipment. "The body is a machine made by the hand of God," Easterday had replied, "infinitely better than any machine of human invention." A quotation from Descartes, he'd said; but the sentiment, Teller realized now, had come straight from Easterday's heart. The doctor's eye was aimed beyond organ and tissue, cell and chromosome, molecule, plasma, helical DNA. A mechanic of the corpus, Easterday aspired to Romance.

Teller spoke in open amazement. "You're in love with her."

"The question is," the doctor, dropping his eyes, seemed a shy fat boy of fifty, "are you?"

"She's my wife."

Easterday make a smacking sound with his lips.

"Am I in love with Nina?" Teller rose from his perch. "I am."

"You are—truly?"

"Heart and soul," he declared.

"Ah, a closet Quixote." The doctor's voice, barely audible, sounded no mockery. His slow smile seemed Buddha-like. "There's hope for you after all."

Teller captured one of Easterday's soft paws in his hands and warmly squeezed it. "Thank you." His heart went out to his physician. "You're a good man."

Easterday slid free. "Please."

Embarrassed by his overflow of emotion, Teller faced the door. After a moment, pink-cheeked, he turned back. Easterday's look stopped his hand on its way to his wallet. "No," Teller said, "I won't insult you."

"Good." The doctor had assumed his swivel seat, the desk a barrier of pale oak emphasizing his authority. "Your wife is here for her regular physical. I'm afraid I've kept her waiting too long already."

For twenty-eight minutes Teller endured the auger of doubt. He leaped to his feet as Nina reentered the waiting room. "You're all right?"

"Yes," she said. "Are you?"

"Of course."

"Why were you so upset? Is there really something wrong with your heart?"

"Only a misunderstanding."

They stepped from the office into a swirl of white flakes. When Nina offered her hand, he accepted it as a token of the gift of herself.

Smoker

No? No! You said *No?*"

"Yessir!" I shout, keeping my eyes on the eagle-anchor-globe emblem centering his Smokey the Bear hat and for all I know pinned straight back into his brain.

"Maggot, you messing with your drill instructor's mind?"

"Nossir!" I shout all my replies. It indicates esprit de corps. "Sir, Private Troy is just not a fighter."

Sergeant Schramm smacks me open-handed, but hard, alongside the head. "I've got no room for pussies in this platoon. A marine is a fighter. You hear me?"

"Yessir."

"What is it with you, Troy? You want to screw up this platoon?"

"Nossir." But I want nothing to do with Company B's smoker bouts and Sergeant Schramm's dreams of glory. He got his other volunteers quick enough—proof that your average USMC boot has all the brain power of a Doberman.

"Well, your drill instructor is going to kick your big dumb ass for you unless you stand up and fight for this platoon. You understand, maggot?"

"Yessir."

There are sixty-nine other recruits standing at attention before their racks, each one staring straight ahead as though stone-deaf, stone-blind. *"The Marines Are Looking For a Few Good Men."* They must still be looking.

"Therefore, maggot, you're volunteering. Understand?"

"Yessir."

"Let me hear it."

"YESSIR!"

He smacks me again. "Say it, dummy! All of it."

"Sir! Private Troy is volunteering to fight in the smoker bouts for the honor of platoon one sixty-nine, sir!" I shout it out, standing tall. Since there's no room for pussies in this platoon, I look the brave gyrene as I give in.

Schramm's eyes scan me as if checking for concealed weapons, or maybe he's trying to read my mind for subversive thinking. A college boy's got to be a potential Commie. I don't move a hair of what little's left on my skull. The first couple of weeks at Parris Island I got my ass kicked royally for slouching. Taller than most of the platoon, I'm easy to spot. But now I got it down pat: I do this dynamite imitation of a dummy.

Though I'm still getting my fair share of harassment. Either my general attitude bugs him, or Schramm likes to pick on guys his own size and I'm the only one in the platoon who fills the bill—except for Mongon, the Zombie from Altoona, who doesn't, and can't, count.

Schramm leans his face very close to mine. His breath smells of mint over chili. "Let me tell you something you wise-ass fat-assed asshole." When flustered, our sergeant is subject to fits of redundancy. "Not only will you fight, but you will win. Understand?"

"Yessir." 'Win' is a holy word to Schramm. 'Marines are winners,' he's fond of screaming. I don't mention Vietnam. Nor the fact that since I slid into the Corps on my drift out of school, I tend to see the boot as a loser.

"You lose, you disgrace this platoon. You disgrace this platoon, you disgrace your drill instructor. You want to disgrace me, maggot?"

70

"Nossir!" I want to erase him, or escape him.

"All right." He looks regretfully at Mongon, then at Hogevar who goes one-eighty but is all sausage. He sighs. A man's choices are so limited. "You're our heavyweight, Troy."

The next morning after chow Schramm excuses the boxing team from close order drill so we can go to the gym. "Sergeant Gharrity will give you some pointers, help give us an edge."

Sergeant Gharrity is a quiet type with a little sandy mustache. He looks us over without any apparent excitement at discovering real prospects. There's Cruz the lightweight; our jive-ass welter who fantasizes he's Ali; Payne, a stringy-muscled chocolate-colored middleweight; Sabota with legs like a Budweiser horse; and me.

The coach shows us how to wrap our hands, then tosses me a pair of old bag gloves. They smell like pussy. I shove my hands into them, and go from peanut to bolo to heavy bag, working up a sweat. I can triple up on jabs and hook off the jab. My right hand I use for balance so I don't tilt when I walk.

Gharrity stands at ease eyeballing me. He's so calm he reminds me of Archie Moore. After a time he stops me and tosses the bag gloves to Sabota, then asks me to hold out my hands. Even taped, they're small. I've got long thin fingers too: great violinist material.

"Corporal Johnson," Gharrity calls. A paunchy, yellow black guy gets into the ring. He's a light-heavy who should train down to middle. The coach laces me into a pair of pillow gloves. "Let's see what you got," he says.

I get into the ring and slip around the slick canvas with Corporal Johnson without either of us doing undue damage to each other. The corporal likes to dart in and out. He lands a lot but his punches are slaps. Slappers don't have power.

I tattoo his forehead with jabs as he's coming and going. It bothers him. If I did it nonstop for fifteen rounds it might give him a migraine. If my arm didn't fall off first.

Time is called and the Slapper and I tap gloves. *Semper Fi* and all that. I wish I could draw him in the tournament.

Gharrity unlaces my gloves and flips them to Sabota. "Where'd you learn to jab like that?"

"Sir, my Dad."

"He was a fighter?"

"Yessir." I meet his eyes, but he doesn't seem to mind. "He was a fighter."

He nods. His eyebrows are traced with little silvery lines. I wonder if he had a good cut man. Ikey Leviton had Dad's cuts stopped almost as soon as his butt hit the stool. Dad gave Ikey plenty of practice.

"You don't use your right."

"Sir, I'm saving it." I keep a straight face.

He looks at me like he knows me from someplace. "You want to save something, start a bank account." He tells me to skip rope, do push-ups and sit-ups, then turns to watch Sabota and the Slapper. The Slapper's crowding Sabota so he can't wind up and blast him. Sabota backpedals to get room, but tangles his feet and lands on his ass.

I find a rope and some space. Dad sparred with me on the back porch. He could've destroyed me, but never once hurt me; he only wanted to teach me self-defense. If a man can stand up for himself, he said, he can have pride.

He also told me, after stopping to compliment me on my footwork or my left, that I ought never to have anything to do with prizefighting. It was a dying way of life, though it happened to be his.

And he told me to throw my right. But sparring, with Dad coming at me in that tight crouch, those layers of scar tissue showing over his gloves, I couldn't let it go.

Gharrity looks at me. I show him a lot of heart skipping rope.

Everybody gets to spar with the Slapper, who must be doing this to lose weight or because he's a masochist, and we all skip rope and hit the bags. Then we run laps around the gym, forward and backward, Sabota falling down a lot backward, and do windsprints at which little Cruz is dynamite.

"You people," Gharrity says, "be here tomorrow." It's clear

he can take us or leave us. I guess to him we must look pretty rank.

The next day I'm sparring when our platoon's D.I.'s walk in: Schramm, Bandle, and Lane, a vigilante law firm. They must have chipped in for a babysitter to watch the Dobermans.

"Use the right," Schramm starts yelling. I keep slipping around, jabbing, obviously trying to get through all this with the least possible pain. Schramm pounds on the ring apron. "Use your right, Troy. That's an order!" So of course when I do throw it, the Slapper's waiting and whacks me a stinging hook on the ear.

"Time!" Gharrity calls.

"Goddamnit, Troy, you had best shape up."

Bandle and Lane chime in with Schramm. "You heard your drill instructor, maggot." "You better show us some balls in there, boy." They get the harmony down, they'd make a nifty trio.

"He's got a good left," Gharrity says with the enthusiasm of a man ordering a cup of coffee.

"He's got shit!" Schramm drags me to the heavy bag. "You hit that with your right, maggot, just the right. Do it."

I do it.

"You lose and your ass is grass, you understand?"

"Yessir."

"My platoon is going to win that smoker. Understand?"

"Yessir."

Sergeant Schramm is a winner; his platoons are winners. Our platoon was number one on the rifle range. Schramm even got Mongon the Zombie to qualify by repeated beatings about the skull area. Fear is a terrific motivational factor. Schramm scared us so totally witless that we were real mean mothers in the weekend field meets. And the way he's got us roboting about, hup, hup, hup, we're a cinch to cop the drill trophy. So of course he wants the smoker bouts. A winner doesn't want to foul up his record.

Like when Uncle Jack the Realtor got Dad a night watchman job after his fighting was finished. "Just don't screw it up, Ernie, okay? You screw it up, it's a blot on my reputation, you see what I'm saying?"

Uncle Jack the Realtor always talked to my Dad as though he wasn't sure if his words were penetrating the cauliflower crop. Jack wore gold tie-clips and cufflinks with his initials, and always had a club pin of one kind or another in his lapel. He jingled keys and coins in his pocket when he talked to you.

Jack was my mother's brother and seemed to feel some responsibility for Dad and me after she left. Maybe he advised her to split and marry the pharmacist who'd give her security, I don't know. But Jack would drop by the apartment every so often, checking up on us like we were a couple of kids on our first camping trip.

When Dad died—at forty-two he was as hard as knuckles but had an enlarged heart bigger than his fist—Jack offered to get me a night job so I could finish my last year of college. I think he was worried about me because I'd stopped going to classes, or maybe because every time my mother called I'd hang up on her.

It wasn't like I wasn't keeping myself occupied. I watched a lot of TV, soaking up the soaps until I thought I'd drown in all the drinks and tears that went with those screwed-up lives. Every so often I'd punch the peanut bag on the back porch, or when I needed it most land a haymaker on the living room wall. That wall looked pretty bad when I got finished with it; my hands didn't look so great either.

Uncle Jack said I was making a terrible mistake not taking his advice. "You're not dumb, Billy. You get that sheepskin." Jingle, jingle. "You'll be better off."

Better off than whom we both knew. I told him thanks, but I thought I'd take this terrific offer from the government.

"The right," Schramm yells. "The right!"

"Yessir." Bam, bam. I'm really putting hurt on that bag.

The smoker's on Friday and Saturday nights. Friday I draw a bye. I watch Cruz get waltzed around and outpointed by a spidery black kid. He comes back and sags on the metal chair next to me. The cigar smoke from the front row brass is enough to make you cry. Cruz is crying, but it's because the poor guy had his heart set on winning. "I coudn get off, I coudn get off," he keeps saying, one nostril leaking blood.

Schramm appears briefly to inform Cruz he's a worthless sack of shit.

"You did the best you could," I tell Cruz. But there's no consoling him. He hangs down his head, almost to between his knees. Rank with sweat, he smells like the bag gloves in the gym.

Our welter, this cocoanut with an amazing array of bolo punches and blurring Ali flurries, all thrown six inches short of the mark, lasts one minute and eighteen seconds before the stolid bohunk he's entertaining wades in to bomb him with a roundhouse right.

As they haul the welter out, Schramm pushes at his shoulder in disgust. Schramm is such a terror, I think maybe I ought to offer him my place in the ring.

Payne, our middleweight, is lucky like me and has a bye. Sabota, who learned in training that he can't run backward, runs forward. He bulls the heart out of a Mexican kid who sits down in the middle of round two and stays sitting. Schramm goes berserk slapping Sabota on the back.

And then we watch the heavyweights. Platoon 168's man is a gleaming ebony god of muscle. What 170 has to offer up as sacrifice is a squat, blocky guy named Levine from Philadelphia. Levine leaps up at the bell. He's one of these hyperactive types, hitting himself in the head, flapping his elbows, chewing his mouthpiece, hopping, doing weird little Disco dips and twists, and swinging from his toes with everything. While we all sit with our mouths hanging open, the tower of ebony crumples once, twice, and the third time is counted out. And carried out. And is still out.

Payne looks at me, "Shee-it, man," shaking his head.

In the squad bay afterwards, Schramm is in a state. He paces up and down with us at attention, yelling and shaking his fist. I'm relieved to see that he's not frothing at the mouth.

"You maggots see Sabota, you see what he did?"

"Yessir!"

"He won because a marine only knows one way to go—forward. A marine does not know the meaning of the word retreat. A marine does not know the meaning of the word fear."

I figure there's a lot of words a marine doesn't know the meaning of, independence, for instance, or tranquility, but I don't mention it.

"I seriously doubt that any of you pussies will ever be marines! You know that?"

"Yessir."

"Especially you, Cruz! And you," he screams at the KO'd welterweight. He smacks the two losers. "You make me sick. Get down, both of you. Give me ten."

They hit the deck and crank out push-ups. The rest of us are stone.

"And another ten. And ten more. And keep it up till you drop." He tells Sergeant Bandle to take over the platoon. "Payne! Troy!"

"Yessir." We jump forward, snapping to attention.

"Report to the hut."

I follow Payne on a dead run past the head to the D.I.'s quarters. Schramm comes in to toss down a duffel bag and an entrenching tool. "Fill it with sand. Move."

"Yessir!"

Out back I dig while Payne holds open the bag. Payne looks longingly at the sawgrass swamp behind our barracks. "Shee-it, man," he says mournfully. "Wasn't for them sharks, I swim my sweet young ass away from this hole."

I fill half the bag before switching places with him.

"An I was you," he says, "I swim it with the sharks."

We drag the bag inside. Schramm has us rig it with ropes to hang from a thick overhead steel pipe.

"Just cause you lucked into byes, pussies, don't mean you don't work up a sweat tonight." He hands Payne a pair of U.S. Government issue leather dress gloves and tells him to hit while I hold. Payne bounces around, bapbapbap, battabap. He's quick and snaps his punches so they smack when they land, but holding the bag I can feel he doesn't have power.

"I want a knockout from you tomorrow night, you understand."

"Yessir!" Payne yells, like that's exactly what he was thinking and he is pleased to have this fine gentleman bring up the subject. I lean my cheek against the coarse cloth of the bag so I won't have to meet his eyes.

Schramm has us switch. The gloves are tight on my hands.

"Now you listen to me, maggot. No dancing, no pitty-pat shit. Use the right and use it right. That Jew boy is gonna dismantle your ass you don't nail him early."

From what I saw Levine's going to dismember me unless I use an M-60, but I shuffle around and smack the right against the bag. It's like hitting cement. Payne grunts as though it's hard holding his ground against such shocking force. I appreciate his effort, but Schramm isn't buying.

"Step into it! Use your weight!" He smacks the bag, then me. Equal treatment. "What the hell you holding back for?"

"Sir, I'm not."

"Cute, that's what you are. I got me a cute heavyweight."

Maybe Schramm's right; maybe what I am is cute. When I was sixteen and starting my wise-ass act, Dad kept giving me odd looks like he wasn't sure if he recognized me. He didn't say anything though. I guess he figured everybody had his own style; some were natural southpaws, some were natural wise-guys.

"No guts," Schramm says, "that's your problem, Troy!"

That's a possibility. It was never one with Dad. No sir. It made my throat ache and my balls try to tuck up inside my gut to see him leap, winging that right like it was a discus. I saw him nailed in mid-flight a dozen times if I saw it once. I sat there watching, my hands balled up into helpless little fists, wishing that he wouldn't try so hard, that he would be more defensive.

I remember the fight he had with an Italian kid from Hartford, a comer named Cardelli who was knocking everybody cold: eighteen KO's in eighteen fights.

Lindsey, Dad's manager, took the fight. "What can we lose?" he actually had the balls to say.

Cardelli hit Dad with everything but his ring stool for ten rounds. Dad was still on his feet at the end, his eyes swollen shut, the size of hard-boiled eggs, the tight hot skin gone purple. When he grinned his teeth filmed with blood. "Kid couldn't put me away," he said.

To me, he looked horrifying and beautiful. I'd have kissed him if I wasn't afraid it would hurt too much. I wished my mother was there to see his face, but of course that was the reason she wasn't there.

And on the way to the dressing room some drunk yelling, "You lost, you bum!" tried to sucker-punch Dad. I went for the creep, but Ikey shoved him out of the way. Dad paid it no mind. Like he was blind or something.

When Dad finally quit fighting I felt guilty to feel so relieved. He took it in stride though, which made it easier on both of us, on me at least. Sometimes he'd spar with me, but not as much as before. I was bigger than he was by then. I was starting college and he was working nights, and we didn't get much time together. I always packed him a good lunch for work. He carried it in a black dinner pail to the paper box factory where he watched all night for his employer and never once let anything bad happen to the paper boxes.

"You hear me?" Schramm screams.

"Yessir!"

"Then hit that bag!"

I shuffle around, banging the bag with the right, hard too, making Payne fight to hold it. No hand wrap, no proper glove. Bam, ba-bam. Sergeant Schramm smiles, no doubt congratulating himself on another fine job of making a man out of a boy. "At ease, maggot."

I stand there sweating. Schramm pops me one in the shoulder and says that's how I'm to handle Levine tomorrow night.

After lights out, I get out of the rack and dig my mess kit from my haversack. I take out the folding utensils and go into the head. Tapping the spoon against the top of the middle finger of my right hand, I get a jolt of pain in the second joint where it's cracked. The spoon trick was Dad's; he'd had every one of his fingers broken a couple of times at least.

But I figure what the heck, I don't use it anyway.

The next night we three survivors from 169 sit on metal chairs and witness platoon 170's lightweight and welterweight demolish their assigned targets. That's it for 168.

Payne takes his turn. Discovering some class in himself, he ignores Schramm's screams to "Put him away!" and sticks and moves sweetly enough to take the decision. He comes back all sweat and grin, the muscles in his long chocolate legs jumping, and I slap him ten on his hand-wraps. My right hand jerks with the impact, but he doesn't notice. He's trembling all over like a horse after a race. His teeth keep flashing one message: it's so *good* to win.

Sabota rushes out to meet his opponent and they clash in ring center, back up, and collide again like rams in heat. Halfway into the round they bang heads and Sabota's man gets lit up, his right brow split wide open. Despite protests of a butt, Sabota wins a TKO.

Rival chants—"169! 169!" and "170! 170!"—start up, but nobody tells the boots to knock it off. The cigar-puffing brass are in an indulgent mood; let the boys have their fun.

Schramm motions to me and I hulk my way down the aisle to the ring. He halts me at the base of the steps. "You win this one," he says, "or I will personally . . ."

I step up away from him while he's talking. I'll pay for it later, but right now I don't give a damn.

The corner men assigned to me, two gangly creeps who look like lifetime lance corporals, check my tapes. They hold out the twelve ounce gloves and I jam my left into one, then wriggle the right gingerly into the other.

The announcer is mouthing off at the mike about the final

event. "Representing plah-tooon wan-sixty-nine!" He really gets off on the nine, as though it meant something special. The Dobermans howl and bark. "From Dee-troit, Michigan . . ."

That was the way Dad said Detroit. Ernie Troy, the Dee-troit Destroyer, 48–21–0. Destroyed his way right up the rankings to just below the top ten—at which point class middleweights started destroying him. And at which point Lindsey, that jerk!, should have dropped him back down in competition, but the purses were bigger up there, and he wasn't the one getting nailed.

"Weighing one hundred and ninety-six pounds! Private Billy Troy!"

Nice touch, that private bit. So we don't get mixed up with all the sergeants and majors in here getting their brains scrambled. I give the pack a catchy little flick of my left glove and they absolutely love it, pounding their paws raw.

After Private Richie Levine at two-oh-eight from the City of Brotherly Love gets properly introduced to the mob, we saunter out to touch gloves and hear the ref tell us to obey his commands at all times, and don't dog it.

Levine tries the Liston glare so I blow him a little kiss. We go back to our corners, rolling our heads, fluttering our arms, then the bell rings.

Levine swats himself up alongside the head harder than it looks like I'll be able to hit him, and comes out, flapping and hopping, chomping on the mouthpiece, dipping and twisting. It's disco time.

He's getting me tired just watching him, so I sidle forward to bounce a couple jabs off his forehead. But it's like stepping into a meat-grinder. He's all over me, punching and butting and shouldering me into a corner. I try to slide away but he pushes me open-handed back into the ropes: you stay where I put you, mother, so I can work on you. Which he does. Disco here, disco there, he puts them wherever he wants them, which is anywhere as long as it's on me, my elbows, hips, shoulders.

I'm glad I'm wearing a cup. I'm glad he's wearing a mouthpiece; he might try to chew off an ear when he's in close.

I roll along the ropes, roughing my shoulders, and find a new corner. My prospects do not improve. The cheers are turning to boos. I peek out of my gloves once in a while to make sure it's only one guy out there.

The bell breaks off the barrage and the boos. I manage to saunter back to my corner. I let my mouthpiece fall out and don't toss my cookies.

"He's getting tired," one of the corner creeps says.

"Really? Ask him if he wants to throw in the towel. I'll understand."

Schramm is screaming for me to use the right, to win, to do something.

I rinse my mouth, spit pink water and don't get up until the bell. The Disco Kid zips out looking for his partner, edging left to cut off my retreat. I surprise him by moving to his right, into his power, and bing him on the ear with a hook.

That displeases him. He roars off the ropes. I catch his bombing rights and slaughterhouse hooks on my elbows and shoulders, leaning into him to smother his power, then slip free and back-pedal, jabbing like crazy. He bangs in a couple of hooks which land behind my elbows and kidneys. My mouth falls open, the rubber hanging out, and he butts me under the chin, then shoves me into the ropes and nails me with a straight right as I'm coming off.

Sitting down feels so sweet. Nobody's hitting me. I let my arms dangle at my sides, my gloves at rest on the canvas. It'd feel even sweeter to stretch out and nap until they turn off the lights and all go marching home.

I get to one knee, and push myself up. The referee checks my eyes and asks if I want to go on. "You bet," I tell him.

The Disco Kid's moving to the beat. I'm willing to dance but I don't like him pawing me, so I play coy and slide away.

I lie to him with my left hand, promising to jab as he closes, then bend the jab into a hook. It sets him back on his heels. If I had any power I'd have decked him. As it is, I draw a roar from the Dobermans: hey, our maggot's gonna kick ass!

Jab, jab, jab and I'm away and he's coming and by the end of the round he's got me curled up like a hedgehog hoping those snapping hounds will get bored and go away.

I wobble to the stool. My nose is bleeding and I'm swallowing blood. I'll be leaking it too from those whacks in the kidneys.

The corner creeps tend to me in funereal silence.

At the bell Levine rushes out to drop me with a one-two. I sit down in my corner with my arms draped over the middle strand. I sure as hell don't owe Schramm or the pack anything. Not my life anyway.

The Disco Kid is eyeballing me from a neutral corner. I see he knows he's got me. He even flashes me a white rubber smile. I'm cute; I'm his piece of cake.

The ref drops his arm for eight. I get to my feet.

Levine storms in and I throw a right lead with my shoulder and hip into it, landing high on his forehead. It drops him to his knees.

I dance my way to a neutral corner, trying to look like Killer Billy Troy. Tears are streaming from my eyes; the pain shooting through my right hand up my arm into my shoulder almost makes me puke. My legs are quivering. Actually, I'm too far gone to look dangerous, so try for gutsy.

And the human hurricane, this hyperactive mother who's probably the Philly heavyweight Golden Glove champ with a record of 20–30 KO's and 2 or 3 DOA's, he shakes his head and gets up at three.

Three? Shit! I'm dancing and jabbing and he bangs me into a corner, out of a corner, into another and flat on my back. My head snaps back against the canvas, giving me a great view of the overhead lights with lots of little bright red squiggles darting around.

I roll over and grab a rope and haul myself up at six. I'm too far gone to think about it. The ref asks me if I want to quit. I shake my head, he wipes my gloves and turns me loose.

Levine attacks and I straighten him up with a stiff-arm jab. When he comes in again, I hold my ground, trading with him, and catch a right on the ear that jellies my legs. I tie him up for a few seconds, push off with my right forearm under his chin, bang a hard left hook into the ribs, and bring it upstairs to land on his jaw. He sags into me and we hug each other like brothers.

That's the way it ends. Staggering to my corner, I collapse on the ropes. Levine gets the decision while they're pulling off my gloves. Platoon 170 goes berserk yelling "We're number one! We're number one!"

I get down out of the ring and am surprised to see Sergeant Gharrity. "Nice fight," he says, "he was tiring." He pats me on the shoulder, "Get to sick bay with that hand," and leaves. A bubble rises from my stomach into my chest. It gives me enough lift to walk tall down the long aisle between rows of Dobermans standing in place, awaiting command.

Sergeant Schramm is not a good loser. I guess he hasn't had enough practice. He's waiting outside the dressing room, and slaps me hard on the right ear, setting it to ringing like an alarm.

"You pussy!" he says, then stops as a lieutenant hurries over to snap him to attention.

"Sergeant, did you strike this recruit?"

"Nossir!" Schramm says. He doesn't shout it like we do, but does spit it out, sharp and clear. A master among dogs, a dog among masters.

"Sergeant, I saw you."

"I slapped him on the shoulder, sir. Congratulating him."

"Private, did your drill instructor hit you?"

"Nossir!"

"Son, I saw him. You can tell me the truth."

He's giving me an intense, caring look. Regulations say D.I.'s aren't allowed to hit boots, although everybody knows they do it. They can get busted for it if they get caught, and officers get promotion points for catching them. It's their little game, with the recruit as football. "Sir," I say. "The drill instructor did not strike Private Troy, sir."

Looking peeved, the lieutenant goes briskly about his business.

Schramm mutters something, then looks at me. I meet his eyes and he raises his hand. I stare at his cap. I didn't expect to see gratitude in his look, not even relief. I had hoped to see recognition.

He leans into my face. "You threw that right one time! One time! After I told you!" If he's noticed how swollen my hand is, the sweaty tapes cutting into the flesh, he doesn't mention it. He does mention that I am a no-good chicken-shit yellow bastard of a loser.

He looks around to make sure the lieutenant is gone. My broken hand curls into a fist and all the power of my body flows into my right arm. I could knock down a wall. It would be a sucker punch though, and I let my arm and hand relax.

Schramm starts in on me again. He's got so many words for loser, he must sit up nights studying his Thesaurus. But it all blows by me. Now I know why Dad could grin. He kept his own score.

To think of all that yapping I did. Tell Jack how it is, tell Lindsey, make them see, yap, yap, yap. And when Dad held his peace, I'd been foolish enough to think he was a fool.

"You think you're really something, don't you, Troy?"

Light and bouncy, I show the sergeant my bloody teeth.

Local Anaesthetic

Owen has a cigar and sugared coffee for breakfast. Stuck to the lime green refrigerator door with a plasticized magnet shaped like a strawberry is a list written in Katherine's tiny hand, her webby connections:

> Dr. McGrail, RX
> exterminator?
> Maureen

She is still asleep in the master bedroom. He has taken to sleeping in Maureen's room so his tossing and turning and sweat-soaked pillows do not irritate her. He dials Mark's number on his porta-phone as he paces the kitchen, and gets a recording: Hello, this is Clean Sweep. I'm not available right now. When is he? Owen would like to know. At least the kid has some business sense, if not much of a business. Owen has offered his son the Campus Laundrette or the video game parlor, but Mark always says no. Owen is not about to mention the letter on tape and hangs up without speaking. He rinses his cup. He wants to slip out before Katherine wakes. Not that he fears a lecture, for she seems to have given up on that. Since her mastectomy, she's drawn into herself. Although at fifty Katherine is still a striking woman, her tall lean figure proof of what money can provide in dance and music and eastern college polish, he's let her go without a struggle. He's learned that they get along better at a distance.

In the attached four car garage he wedges past the riding mower, snow blower, snowmobile, Katherine's Peugeot, and his mint-condition lemon-yellow '33 Packard convertible that he drives every year in the vanguard of the Independence Day parade. He takes pride in the fact that Miss Hayes County always rides with him, although with his cronies he shrugs it off as cheap public relations.

His white Coupe DeVille sits in quiet, seeming innocence and for a moment he enjoys the hope that the accident was only a drunk's bad dream. He walks around front to face it. The right fender is bent in against the tire, its headlight aimed cockeyed at the sky. He tries his strength against the metal but it's too much for him. He still doesn't remember what he hit, though he remembers Mark driving him home. How did his son get back to town? It occurs to Owen that Mark might be sleeping in his old room, and he considers going in to check, but doesn't. Mark, an early riser, would be up by now. Owen runs his puffy hands over fender and bumper and again is relieved by the absence of blood. There is a fleck of yellow paint like a scab on the fender. A guard rail, he thinks. He sees a yellow post coming at him, bright in the lights, and tries to convince himself that it is a memory. But in truth all he knows for certain is that he doesn't know. He squeezes into the Caddy, fingers the genie to lift the door, and swings down the long curving drive. The right front tire rubs, like a prisoner groaning in his sleep. He'll have new rubber put on all the way around. Another fresh start.

On the way to town he notes each shotgun-punctured deer crossing sign, each baseball bat-smashed mailbox and suffers dread of the world's dangers. Owen has never fired a gun. Nor has he ever struck another person, except for the spankings it was his duty to give Mark. His brother Earl loved fighting, but Owen shrank from it. Yet he was a tiger for debate, and rival lawyers complimented him on his instinct for the jugular. It's a cutthroat trade, he told them. What did they expect?

Although they had moved to the country for peace and quiet, he thinks now they ought to move back to town. Katherine would be nearer the hospital, and they could stop in more often on Maureen. There was something to be said too for safety in numbers, for not having your house set up in an unfenced field on a dark road, an invitation to pillage. In town he could walk or take a cab and give up driving before he killed someone and was put away or rammed a pole and left himself a spineless lump. Yet Olentangy's spring-sagging cabs were commanded by young long-hairs he took to be Vietnam vet time-bombs, or by toothless hillbillies wearing reflector sunglasses day and night and looking like escapees from a detox center.

He depresses a chromed lever to lower the windows. The late May air evaporates his clammy sweat. Two figures in silky purple shorts and gold shirts jog toward him: a man and a woman, running abreast of each other. The roads are full of runners now. What I want to know, he asks the mid-morning coffee bunch at the Ease On Inn, is what are they running from? He steers left, giving the joggers a wide berth. You can never tell when one might stumble into your path and land you in court.

Unprovoked, tears flood his eyes. What in God's name is happening to him? He thinks of the farmer's daughter whose family estate he'd settled that winter, a mulish woman who said of her father, things just wore him to a fragile. He snaps open his gold lighter and sets fire to a Mexican Excalibur as thick as his thumb. The smoke nourishes him and he coughs harshly, delighting in the vigorous noise. In town he passes the Hayes County *Sentinel*, a daily that was founded as a weekly by Katherine's great-grandfather, Bennett Nichols. Katherine's brother, Bennett IV, the publisher, on the board of the college and the hospital, is a stiff little prick who never has more than a nod for Owen. The secret of success, Owen confides in a low palaver to his drinking buddies, is to marry money.

He thinks to stop at, then passes by, his own main street office, *Owen Moore, Attorney at Law* in gilt lettering on a stained oak shingle. A familiar pressure starts up behind his eyes. He'd expected Mark to go to law school, and had planned to have a new shingle made, *Moore and Moore*, but Mark never finished college. Owen is painfully disappointed in his son, and that disappoints him in himself as a father.

In the same block is Sherman's Realty with its braggart three-foot-high white sign loud with red lettering: *We Sell the Earth.* And his mother too if there was a buck in it, Owen thinks, bitter with disdain for yappy Robby Sherman. He needs to see Sherman about the Prudential deal, but fears Viva might be there or that Sherman will mention her. Owen's face more and more betrays his feelings.

Mark's apartment is on a side street above a shoe repair shop. New soles and heels. Owen parks and rings the bell, but gets no answer. He steps around the corner and goes down two blocks to Earl's. Mark's old red truck is parked at the curb, two sliding aluminum ladders strapped to the aluminum hop cap. White plastic signs on the cab doors read *Clean Sweep.*

Earl is holed up in the basement of a run-down four-story brick. The building, which Owen owns, sticks out like a decayed tooth between Fidelity Loan and the new Sears catalogue store. Half the tenants are on welfare and collecting the rent is a monthly grief. Owen will be glad to be rid of it.

Although he has a pass key, he knocks. Earl opens the door. "Well, speak of the devil!" He is dressed in shiny blue trousers and a boiled white shirt buttoned at the neck. Tall and stringy, he has a slight leftward lean to his stance, even when sober. Often Owen has seen his brother out on the town, walking uphill on a flat street. Although he appears sickly, Earl is a whip of a man, a welterweight too mean for booze to lick. Sixty pounds heavier, Owen retains his boyhood fear of his older brother. "How's tricks?" he asks. There is a blue-green stub of a veteran's compensation check sticking out of Earl's shirt pocket. It's the tenth of the month; usually Earl would have blown the check by now. He holds a white cup in one hand, and Owen takes note that it does not smell of spirits.

"Mark's here."

"Is he?"

He follows Earl into the bleak, but rent-free, quarters. The concrete floor is chill and damp. Behind the plywood partitions forming the apartment's rear wall are water heaters and a coal conversion furnace which needs replacing. Earl's belongings are stacked neatly on shelves made from melon crates.

Mark, sitting at a card table, looks up from a checkerboard. "How you feeling, Dad?"

"With my fingers," Owen says.

Even inside Mark wears the black top hat and long red scarf of the chimney sweep. His brown beard is long and curly. It shocks Owen to see his son looking like Abe Lincoln. Owen worries there is something seriously wrong with him. "Can I talk to you?"

"Sure," Mark says.

He can't talk about the letter in front of Earl. "How soon you think you'll be done here?"

"We're on the second game."

"Gotta play the rubber," Earl says. "You want some coffee?"

"No. Don't stop your game."

Earl sits at the table. Mark says it's his move. Earl studies the board, then moves. "King me," he says, and turns to Owen. "What brings you down here?"

"I wanted to thank Mark for driving me home last night."

"Don't mention it," Mark says.

Owen waits to see what move his son will make. He hates to think Mark is losing. And he hates being odd man out. "You think it over yet?" he asks Earl.

"What's that?"

"What we talked about."

Earl shrugs. "This here's okay by me."

"Too damp."

"Don't bother me."

"It'll give you rheumatism."

"Give it to me?" Earl laughs, his dentures clicking. He wiggles his fingers as though to demonstrate something, then sticks both fists out over the board beneath Mark's chin. His hands are lumpy and gnarled. "Broke that one cold-cocking a wop up in Toledo. That one twice on Davey Steele. Stainless Steele they called him. He got a shot at Griffith for the title. Got his ass whipped good. I was all the time breaking my hands. Brittle bones. Quinn had to shoot novocaine into the knuckles for me. Local anaesthetic. You're hurtin, you just don't know you're hurtin."

Owen spots a move Mark can make to lock in Earl's king. He knows better than to mention it. He watches with alarm as his son slides a checker into position to be taken. Mark loves to lose. Owen understands so little about his son. Why did he think that he could confide in him? And to leave her letter with him, to give him a weapon to use against his father!

"I'd offer you a snort," Earl says, "but the cupboard's bare as a baby's ass."

Owen reaches for his wallet, then recalls the uncashed check. "You quit?"

"Six weeks," Mark says.

"Kid's got me on carrots and bran." Hunching his shoulders, Earl brings his fists to the ready. "Like training."

Owen arches his eyebrows. "You'll be making a comeback. The senior olympics."

"He's been tapering off since Christmas," Mark says.

"Kidneys need a break." Earl jumps Mark's checker. "So how about you?"

"On and off." Owen winks. "During the week I'm on the sauce, weekends I'm off the wagon." He holds his grin although Mark's disgusted shake of his head hits him like a kick in the family jewels. "Well boys, gotta run. I'm not retired yet. Not like you two." Let the kid have a taste of his own medicine. "I'll call you later," he tells Mark, and at the door calls to Earl, "Give it some thought."

"Already did."

"This weekend I'll run you over there."

"Never liked trailers. Like tin cans."

"Be good for you. Fresh air. You can put in a garden. You'll help him, won't you, Mark?"

His son looks up from the board. "You know what I think."

"Grow potatoes and corn. Be a gentleman farmer."

"I like it here."

You ought to be damned glad you're not in the county home, Owen nearly shouts. "Saturday," he says, "I'll pick you up." He leaves before his brother or son can argue with him further.

After an hour in the office opening mail, he tells Roz, his leggy secretary, that he has some errands to run and stops off at the Swope's Cafe for a reuben and coffee, and to catch up on the paper and the day's bad news. Then, despite his better judgment, he drives up to the college and parks in a visitor's spot.

He mounts the warped wooden stairs in cavernous Old Main, Olentangy Methodist's churchy stone hall, where Viva tutors foreign students in English. Her liquid voice escapes her office, offering tips on avoiding agreement errors. He perches on a wooden student's chair in the high-ceilinged hall. Fraternity symbols are scratched and inked into the surface of the chair arm, along with racial slurs and lustful graffiti. When he was a scholarship student here, he took politics and government courses in the building, and swept it nights on his work-study job. For a moment the setting makes him feel young again, then suddenly he feels immeasurably old. Next month he turns sixty. It seems impossible. He has not felt so unbalanced and uncertain since high school when he was heartsick over the prom queen.

A door opens and a dark young man steps into the hall. Short and square shouldered, he pulls on a brown leather jacket. His trimmed mustache is as dark as oil. He is a Libyan, Viva's said, who makes no effort to conceal his contempt for women teachers. The student passes Owen with no sign of acknowledgment. His walk is a display of male power. It pains Owen to consider how the Libyan must see him, a blubbery small town capitalist with

93

a clown's red nose and cry-baby eyes. Owen's heart swells anew with gratitude for the grace of Viva's love. He lives in fear that at any moment she might snap from her trance and see him for the toad he knows he is.

He hoists himself out of the tight chair and slips down the hall to tap at her door. "Ye-es?" she says, a two note musical call.

He pokes his face in at the crack of the door. "It's only me."

She rises in a green, flowing dress, a plump litle woman as soft as a sweet roll. How can anyone resent her? She wears a yellow silk scarf around her neck. His fingers ache to idly tie and untie it as he has done while lying beside her in a motel bed, the scarf her single item of clothing, their moist bodies cooling down. She leads him by a sleeve into the windowless cubicle and shuts the door. On the white wall behind her a poster urges him to *Support Your Local Rhetorician.* "You shouldn't come here," she says. "I've told you." She allows him one kiss, chaste and avuncular. "What's wrong with you, Owen? You look simply awful."

"Your letter," he says, and sits in the metal chair facing the desk.

"You showed it to her? You didn't."

He doesn't know if it's excitement or fear in her voice. She's too daring for him. She appears to know exactly what she wants, *him*, though why he doesn't know, and seems unafraid of taking risks to get him. Part of him wishes he could match her courage; another part damns the day they met.

She takes her teacher's seat. The desk becomes a formal bar between them. "Did you?"

"I wouldn't do that." Her *out* box is layered with papers; her *in* box efficiently empty. "Mark," he says, "I showed it to him."

"Why?"

"I don't know. I was drinking."

"You promised me you'd stop."

"I will. How can I?" He holds up his empty hands. "All this?"

"I have a student. Can I see you later?"

He shakes his head. He is always telling her no. "Not today."

"Robby said he wanted to talk to you."

In alarm he asks, "What about?"

"I thought you knew."

He nods. "I've got to see him." He is reluctant to leave her and delays getting up. "It's just business." Viva has the softest, gentlest hands Owen's ever known. When she strokes the back of his neck, the corded tension drains away. Once after visiting Maureen, he broke down and cried in Viva's arms. She accepted it as if it were only natural. She is the only person who truly knows him, he thinks. The others know the buffoon who's good for a laugh. Katherine, he feels certain, only tolerates him. Or tolerates the outrageous character he's become for the sake of the man she married.

"Owen, really."

He stands up. "I'm going. I'm sorry." He doesn't feel out-rageous. He feels cautious. Despite his consuming need for Viva, he's been keeping away from her. It's too dangerous for them to meet, Robby is bound to find out, they chanced scandal. Viva is only forty. People would think Owen an old fool. Not for the world would he choose to hurt Katherine by publicly shaming her, although he does not say this to Viva.

"Please, Owen."

"I'll be in touch." He bows out. In the hall he passes a tiny Oriental girl clasping her books to her chest, her smile a bouquet of good cheer.

At his office Roz has a message for him. Mark called. "You should talk to him."

"I do. I try."

She looks up from her word processor. "He worries about you."

"I worry about him." Owen tells her to hold his calls, unless it's Mark, and retreats to his paneled office. He phones Sherman to tell him things are moving along, though there may be a hitch, temporarily, in the Prudential deal. "Hitch?" Robby yaps. "What's with the hitch?" He said temporary, Owen says. "We sit on this," Sherman says, "we lose it." Which means he'll line up something else and put Owen, owner of the target property, out in the cold. Owen does not really want to do business with Sherman, not after what Viva's told him about her husband's cruelties, but neither does he want Sherman to think that he is losing his edge. Even if he is.

At the end of a work day in which all he accomplished was a nap, Owen stops at Just Desserts for cookies. Lova Grooms, Viva's slimmer twin, a spinster, runs the sweet shop. Owen's trouble would be halved if only he were in love with her instead of Viva. She puts a half-dozen chocolate chips into a waxy white bag. Lova's eyes keep to themselves, and when she accepts his money she shows no sign of knowing his secret.

He drives past Appleseed primary school, a yellow sign warning *Slow Children,* to the white Alamo-like care center, Sunny-Vue. He shares the cookies with Maureen. She eats them in such eager enjoyment that he wonders if she really is behind the rest of them, or ahead. But only for a moment. The blank look in her milky eyes shows she is clearly behind. He has to look away from her to the tiled floor. There was no record of retardation in Owen's or Katherine's families, although he worries about Mark and has doubts about Earl, and he fears that Maureen is a judgment upon him. Yet the birth certificate clearly states the umbilical cord was wrapped about the baby's neck. Deprivation of oxygen. Just one of the thousands of accidents that determine a person's life.

When Maureen was still at home she sucked her thumb until the skin was raw. Owen bought her pacifiers. It made Katherine furious, but he didn't stop. What do you mean, he argued, don't encourage her? You want her to make it bleed?

He sits with his daughter until bedtime. Then, although Maureen is old enough to be a mother, he rests a hand on her sweaty, curling hair and sings "I gave my love my cherry," her favorite song. She grabs his hand to suck at the thumb. He does not pull it away, although he is washed in guilt. It is another of his secret satisfactions, and one which he feels is shamefully feminine in a grown man, that he takes such pleasure in her need for his touch. As if this might explain why he has so bravely accepted his daughter being less than normal. People tell him he is an optimist: his wife's illness, his poor girl, his bum of a brother, that he doesn't let it get him down makes them admire his pluck. Owen hides his guilt behind the smile acknowledging their praise. Nobody knows better than a lawyer, he says, there's no such thing as justice.

When Maureen is sound asleep, he retrieves his puckered thumb. How simple it would be to pillow her face and set her free. It has occurred to him too that he could give Katherine an overdose of sleeping pills. And gas himself. Leave the whole shooting match to Mark. Viva would have no trouble finding someone better. There are so many claims on him, and he feels so lacking. It frightens him to be mortgaged to the heart.

He drops by the Elks to play euchre and drink scotch and smoke cigars. It lifts his spirits to feel like one of the boys. He cuts quite a figure in town, and enjoys it. He wears his dove-white hair brushed back in waves to curl at the collar. Winters he goes about in a full length black astrakhan coat and matching hat; spring and summer he sports tailor-made lemon-yellow suits with white shoes, belt, and tie. He snaps off jokes at a rapid-fire rate. Often just a wink or the arching of one bushy brow will crack up his audience. Everyone in Olentangy knows Owen, and he knows everyone of importance. When he wanted new lines painted on his Laundromat lot, a city crew did it for beer. A citizen's group got wind of the deal, but the *Sentinel* ignored the fuss except to print a letter to the editor, and he rode it out in style. He lunches with the chamber of commerce gang. The city manager is his golf partner. He sponsors men's and women's softball teams in the city rec leagues. He MC's the annual cancer benefit. When he was hauled in for failure to control, the hearing was held in chambers. The judge, whose magic act Owen always included in the cancer show, levied a small fine and court costs and afterwards apologized for having to do that much. That Owen, people say, what a character!

He is a character. When he feels low and doubts that he *has* any real character and that that's the reason he's become one, he takes comfort in knowing the fun he provides. Why Mark has become a character, Owen doesn't know.

At midnight he gathers up his nickel ante winnings, announces "It's spring, boys, the sap is rising" and rises, and gets a laugh. He drives to Mark's place. Above the red neon outline of a shoe, lamplight shows in a window. He parks and rings the bell. Mark buzzes him in without asking who it is. Such an easy mark, Owen thinks, a crack he's often used on his son.

The stairs exhaust him. He is puffing and sweating when his son opens the door. "Thought you could duck me, did you?"

"Where's your car?"

"Downstairs. You want me to bring it up?"

"You didn't wreck it, did you?"

"Way I learned to drive was the touch system."

Mark turns his back and Owen follows him into the small living room. He is relieved to see that his son doesn't wear the Lincoln hat at home. The boy is thin in jeans and T-shirt. Owen would make two of him. He shrugs off his yellow jacket and sprawls on the Salvation Army sofa. His white tie flaps up into his face and he slaps it out of the way.

"You want some tea?"

Flattening both palms against his forehead, Owen draws them slowly down over his wet face, then abandons them on the hump of his stomach. Mark has gone out to the nook of a kitchen and stands at the range. When he returns to the living room he is carrying two blue cups. "Here."

Owen sips. "What *is* this crap?" He clunks down the cup, slopping tea onto the rag rug, then struggles to a sitting position. With acute embarrassment he faces the high-backed black rocker he sat in the previous night, naked and steaming from a shower, while his son sponged vomit from his suit. He'd sat there like the village idiot, staring over the horizon of his gut to a penis looking like a thumb left too long in dishwater. You little prick, he'd said, and laughed, getting me into all this trouble. "First," he says, "I want to thank you for last night."

"You already did."

"Did I? Okay, good. So tonight, no bull. Strictly business."

"Mom called. She's worried about you."

"What is this—everybody worrying about me? Something wrong with her?"

"She doesn't know where you are."

"You think I do?" He smirks, and sniffs. "For your information, honest Abe, I went to see Maureen. You can tell your mother that. Maureen the moron." He lifts his chin as though proud of having the nerve to tell the brutal truth. "That's right, your sister's a moron and your old man's a hard ass. So what are you?"

Mark sits in the rocker to drink his tea. Tea and rockers are for old folks. When did Mark get so old? Why did he wear that grandpappy's beard? Did he think it fooled anyone? "Your girl friend here?"

"She's out."

"I mean, she still shacking up with you?"

"I told you, she lives here is all."

Owen rolls his eyes. "Sure, sure." Cissy was a dropout from Olentangy Methodist, a sociology major, Viva said, who'd gotten off the track. When he pushed her on it, Viva said Cissy'd gotten into drugs and had gone through an ugly experience at a fraternity. How ugly? Owen wanted to know, meaning how long of a train did she pull? Viva wouldn't tell him anything else. A pale girl with moony eyes, Cissy held an attraction for Mark that was a mystery to Owen. "You mean you're not screwing her?"

"Don't talk like that."

"You can tell me."

"I don't want to talk about her."

"Why do you have to take in every stray cat comes your way?"

"We're friends," Mark says.

Owen studies his son's face, searching for signs of Maureen's blankness. Something was missing from Mark. When his son was a baby, Owen had gone through a bad time, getting up night after night to strip the boy of his gown and check him for broken bones. Katherine had thought he was losing his mind. But the boy looked so tiny and brittle. Owen feared something would happen to Mark in the night and that he'd end up like his older sister. Katherine made him see a doctor, for himself, and Owen had been given a prescription for Librium which he never got filled. Then, he counted on drink to ease him into sleep; now, drink brought dreams that kept him awake. "You got anything to drink?"

"You ought to take better care . . ."

"Hell, I take care of her, I take care of you, I take care of everybody!"

"Yourself, I was trying to say."

As a teenager Mark preached the virtue of vegetables while Owen feasted on beef. In high school, playing basketball, the boy was a tireless defender who ran the legs off opponents and directed the offense with calm precision. He still held the school record for assists, twenty-three in a conference title game. Owen had urged his son to shoot more. Why are you always passing off? Why don't you ever try to score? "Don't sweat it," Owen says. "I got you in my will."

"That's not what I meant."

"The old man is loaded. And loaded."

"You stoke up all day on coffee and cigars, no wonder you need booze to come down. You're killing yourself."

"So what's insurance for?"

"I can't talk to you when you're like this."

"Oh, you're your mother's boy, all right."

"Give yourself a break, will you?"

"You give me a break! You don't even respect a man's work. You think it's easy hustling a buck? My old man washed windows seven days a week. East side trash, they called us. Shanty Irish and hilligans up from West Virginney. You think you could haul yourself up out of that? No, you've had it all handed to you. So where do you get off sitting in judgment?"

Mark rocks slowly, looking into his cup of tea. The fortune teller.

"So I'm a hard ass. I know that. That's my way. But you tell me, all your wisdom, I mean I've been giving you good advice all these years . . ." Owen turns his head as if addressing a third party. "He doesn't take it, of course, but I keep giving it. Free, too. Come on, your philosophy. Like the donkey said, I'm all ears."

After a time Mark says, "People shouldn't hurt each other."

"What the hell do you think the law is for?" Owen roars. He grunts to his feet, makes it out to the kitchen to open and slam shut cupboards, then veers back to the living room. "Where is it?"

"What?"

"The letter, damnit."

"On the bookshelf."

Owen plucks a sheet of stationery from the brick and board shelving. Having it in his hands calms him a bit. When he found it in his mail at the office, it scared hell out of him. At least Roz had the good sense not to open it. *Owen* was all that was written on the envelope, an ivory envelope like the paper it held; *Owen* in green Flair in Viva's hand, slanted and strong. That was all he needed, for it to get out. He walked a line now between being an eccentric and an outcast, and his steps were more and more unsteady. What did she think she was doing?

He stands, leaning against the wall, reading.

I waited, but you didn't call. I saw you coming out of the Elks then. You know I hate to see you like that. Why must you punish yourself? If it's me, then stop seeing me. Or have you already made up your mind to do that? Why don't you ever call? We don't have to keep up this act. I don't care what anyone thinks. They're our lives, aren't they? Let Robby file for divorce. I have a good lawyer, don't I? When are you going to call me? I miss you, I miss you, I miss you.

Again he's encouraged by the fact that she didn't sign it. He thinks it shows she still has some sense of discretion. But why does she keep hitting him with questions? He's told her time and time again he doesn't have the answer. He sees no way out but to quit seeing her altogether; an impossibility, he knows. "You know her, don't you?"

"I guess."

Owen folds the letter and slides it into a back pocket. "She teaches at the college," he says, as if her position were proof that his feelings for her were serious, and that she were worthy of them. "She's a fine woman. She has the most musical voice."

"I've seen her around."

Mark looks away, and Owen is angered by his son's prissy embarrassment. Like all the young, the boy believes he has a corner on romance. "But you," Owen says, his voice taking on the razor irony that diminishes claims of opposing attorneys, "you're the Bunker Hunt of the heart, right? After all, you've got Cissy, the frat boys' friend."

"Okay," Mark says, "forget it."

"I was a damned fool to show this to you. It's none of your business."

"I didn't ask to see it, did I?"

"Who said you did?" He hadn't been able to stop himself. He'd felt somehow that Mark of all people would be the one to understand, possibly even to forgive him. "So what do you think? Your old man's a bum, that it?"

"It's your life. I can't tell you what to do."

"Will you listen to this guy? He should've been a lawyer." Owen catches an echo of Paddy Tarpy, a buddy of Owen's father, a mick with a brogue who said "loyer" for lawyer and liar. Ah, Paddy would say of a man not to be trusted, isn't he the biggest loyer in town now?

"If you're worried I'm going to say anything, I'm not."

"That's all she needs! Her husband's a jerk. No wonder she wants to dump him. She's gone on me, can I help it?" He violently shakes his head, trembling the soft flesh of his cheeks. "Listen, you've got no idea . . ." Despite himself, he winks. "A man's got to get a little on the side, okay?" He watches his son walk to the window to stand looking out. "Don't worry, I'm not going to bust up things. Who'd take care of your mother? You and Maureen?"

"Dad," Mark says, his back still turned. "What do you want from me?"

"I love your mother," Owen says. He doesn't know what he expects his son to say in reply, but it was true that he loved Katherine. And Viva. Where, he wonders, do we get the idea that love *solves* anything? "Cat got your tongue?" He takes Mark's silence as a sign of disdain. The boy seems so perversely stupid about the real world. Owen knows he has only himself to blame. He's the one who let Earl live with them when Mark was a boy. Katherine never wanted it. But Earl was trying to get back on his feet and, though his stay stretched into a year, kept saying it was only a temporary arrangement. When he was supposed to be hunting a job, he sat at home reeling off stories of his heroic life among the lowly, and playing checkers with Mark. That was the root of the trouble. While the old man was out on the make, dog eat dog, the kid was learning from a loser how to lose. "Forget it. Give me the rest of it and I'll hit the road."

"Rest of what?"

"The copy. Who do you think you're dealing with, some kid?"

"The letter? Dad, that's it."

His son turns to face him. Did he really believe that he would breeze through life by looking innocent? "Come on, I didn't raise any id . . . Look, I'm not blaming you. I was in your shoes, I'd do the same damned thing. Anybody in his right mind would."

Mark shakes his head. "I can't believe you."

"You want to break your mother's heart?" Owen approaches his son until he is close enough to hit him, or hold him. "What, you want to play rough? Kid, your old man's a pro. You remember what happened to the checks?" For a time he sent Mark a monthly check for two hundred dollars, writing it off on taxes as building maintenance. When he discovered Mark signed them over to a Head Start program, he stopped them cold. "Kiss your trust fund goodbye too. And you think I can't write you out of my will? You're talking to a lawyer, buster."

Mark lays a hand on his father's shoulder. Owen pulls away. "You think you'll draw a pension from cleaning chimneys?"

"Dad, I like what I'm doing. It's useful work. I make a living."

"My old man washed windows till the day he died. I know." Owen goes to the door. "I trusted you, my own son, and this is how you pay me back? I know what's behind it. But that dump is downtown property, a prime location. Prudential's hot for it. The trailer, it's a mobile home, it's almost new. Earl's lived in worse. He'll like it." Owen feels himself winding down. He pats his pockets but finds no cigars. He needs a drink. Sometimes it hits him, his weakness and the weight of age, and he goes so flat he can barely move. He doesn't want Mark to see him that way. "Okay, I know when I'm in a bind. Keep the trust fund. I'll start up the checks too. I've been had, okay? You're shrewd, kid. Now hand it over."

"Dad, you ought to see a doctor."

"What is it, you want me to tell Sherman the deal's off?"

"That's your business."

"I'm out of it then, but what the hell. The old man drops a big deal. Big deal, right? Don't stand there like a dummy! Say something."

"You won't listen to me anyway."

"A chip off the old block. And you act like you don't know the score. Okay, kid, you drive a hard bargain. The apartment stays. Your uncle can live in it until he rots. That make you happy?"

"If you really want my opinion," Mark says. "I know he wants to stay there. He gets along with the people. It won't do him any good to be stuck in a trailer where all he has to do is drink."

"Jeez, will you listen to the speech! You and him, some team. Okay, you win." Owen unsteadily crosses the room to claim his yellow jacket. "But that letter ever gets out, I'll sell the damned dump so fast it'll make your head swim. Understand me?" Although Mark doesn't make a move, Owen nods. "Just so we understand each other."

In the hallway he loses his balance and stumbles, running, down the stairs to slam into the door at the bottom. He fumbles it open and steps into the quiet street. He is trying to open his car door when Mark sticks his head out of the window above the neon shoe. His son's face glows pink in the light. "You know there's no copy," Mark calls down. His beard looks to be on fire. "You don't want to put him out. That's the truth."

Owen slams the door. He revs up the engine, then hides his face in his hands, weeping in fear and pride.

Close Dancing

Word came down from Sister Mary Annunciation, their eighth grade teacher and principal of Saint Sebastian's. As usual, it had to do with trouble and Doolan.

Doolan and some guys were rambling through alleys heading home from hardball in the field behind the old Toledo Paper Box factory. Osmanski and Kleinschmidt were playing catch. Tony Pavoni shouldered a Louisville slugger.

Doolan had broken off a limb from a stinkweed tree, Tree of Heaven his mother called it, and stripped it of branches, to use as a walking stick. As a kid, playing Robin Hood or Geronimo, he'd made bows and arrows from stinkweed trees.

The mid-May afternoon sky was robin's egg blue. In two weeks June would free Doolan for good from the gray stone fort of Saint Sebastian's. He would spend the summer working on his uncle's farm. Come September, he'd start high school at Eli Whitney or Christ the King; he hadn't yet made up his mind.

Eddie Reardon, Annie's younger brother, a yo-yo who glued bb's to cherry bombs and winged them at cats, came running up. "She gave 'em hell! She's gonna take 'em to see Father Speer!" He danced about as he talked, his monkey face split with a grin. He was forever pestering Annie. Because Doolan went over to talk to Annie or get help with his English, Eddie told everybody

Doolan and Annie were steadies, though they were just good friends.

"What's going on?" Osmanski demanded.

"Annunciation, she knows all about it. My sister just come home—crying. Annunciation kept her after, her and Louetta Shoemacker. Is she gonna catch it from my old man."

"For what?" Doolan said.

"*You* know. You guys are gonna catch it too."

"I dint do anything," Pavoni said. He looked whipped already. His dad drove a beer truck and used a razor strop on all five of his boys.

"You guys thought you were getting away . . ."

Doolan whacked Eddie on the shins with the stinkweed. Reardon jumped back, grin gone, and Doolan grabbed him by the shirt. "Why'd you tell Annunciation?"

"Wasn't me! I didn't have nothing to do with it."

"Kick his ass," Kleinschmidt said.

"Butt out," Doolan told him. He shook Reardon. "What'd she say?"

"She said it was a mortal sin. She said the girls gotta promise to stop it. They have to go to confession, and . . ."

"You little liar!" Doolan's stomach felt sick. Annie had come home crying? He gave Eddie a shove. "Get outta here."

Reardon ran to the end of the alley. "I'm gonna tell my old man!" he yelled, then lit out.

"You guys know something I don't?" Willie Kleinschmidt licked his loose, pink lips. He was tall and bony, pimpled and ducktailed. His brother Dick, a junior at Eli Whitney, made zip guns in shop and wore a black leather belt with a sharpened steel buckle. Dick bombed around in a primered '51 Chevvie with a blonde tramp named Winky who he said went all the way with him at the passion pit. "Hey, Pavoni," Kleinschmidt said, "you playing stinky finger with Shoemacker?"

"Get lost," Pavoni said. He looked at Doolan and shrugged.

When Doolan lifted the stinkweed limb, Kleinschmidt spread

his hands. "Hey, boppers, hang loose. I just want to know what's happening."

Doolan flipped the limb up the alley. They all knew he wasn't going to beat on Kleinschmidt unless he had to; if he did, Dick would lay for him and royally stomp his ass.

"Goddamn nuns!" Doolan said.

By the time he got home, his mother had left for work. She'd taped a note to the refrigerator: Dennis, you're in trouble for not coming straight home. Get your homework done and write to your Uncle Frank. Warm up the macaroni and cheese. *Turn off* the stove!

Doolan's mother worked second shift as a telephone operator. She'd worked ever since Doolan's father stepped out for a pack of cigarettes and didn't come back. She would divorce that man, she said, if it weren't for the church.

Doolan warmed his meal. He turned on the radio, an old wooden Zenith with torn speaker fabric; it almost drowned out the noise from Maloney's Bar & Grill downstairs. "All I Have to Do Is Dream" was playing and Doolan got up and tried to dance to the music. It was hard dancing alone in the kitchen. It was hard for him with a partner too. Even though Annie had done her best to teach him.

Annie's family had a television set and sometimes he watched it with them. They acted like it was okay for him to hang around. Mr. and Mrs. Reardon were nuts about "Ozzie and Harriet" and "Bishop Sheen." Sometimes Doolan and Annie watched "American Bandstand," but it was no big deal, not like a date or anything.

When he'd eaten and washed the dishes, Doolan wrote a letter to Uncle Frank, saying he'd be ready to work on the farm as soon as school was out. He tried doing his homework, but gave up. It was his fault Annie was in trouble; he was the one who wanted to learn to dance so he wouldn't have to stand around with his hands in his pockets at Dotty Condon's graduation party. Poor Annie. He wasn't really worried about himself. One way or another, he was always in trouble, and was used to it. Annie Reardon, though, might never again show her face at school. She should have known better than to pal around with Doolan.

He had been hauled down to Father Speer twice that year. The first time was after he and Tom Duffy were serving the eight o'clock Mass and Duffy had elbowed Doolan as they were getting the water and wine cruets. At communion, when Duffy crossed behind him with the paten, Doolan kicked at him and Duffy fell. Doolan hadn't meant to trip him, but Sister Petronilla, Annunciation's eagle-eyed henchman, had spotted the action. After Mass Doolan told his side of the story. Duffy said he hadn't done a thing. Duffy was the starting quarterback of Saint Sebastian's football team. Mr. Duffy owned a dry cleaners, was an usher on Sundays, and gave tons of money to the church. Doolan got kicked out of the servers for good. His mother cried. She'd had hopes he might become a priest. Now, she said, she just prayed he wouldn't turn out like his father.

Then, later that year, Annunciation had assigned a story to write for English. Doolan wrote one about a man who acted like he was just an ordinary guy but was really a hero saving people in trouble. The story had a lot of action and when Doolan read it to Pavoni and Annie they said it was awfully good. They thought he should send it to the *Weekly Messenger.* But when he turned it in Annunciation wanted to know what he'd copied it from. His vocabulary and sentence diagram assignments were all C's and D's, yet the story was an A. That proved it wasn't his own work, she said.

Doolan had stood in front of the room and listened like it was no big deal. He didn't try to argue because it wouldn't do any good. Even if he'd asked Annie to tell about the poem he'd written, Annunciation would only say Annie was lying too. Nuns knew kids lied, all kids; they were born knowing it maybe. Besides, he didn't want to bring up the poem in front of the other guys since it was sort of a love poem about this mystery girl: "You must have come from above/To fill our world with beauty and love." And he didn't really want to remind Annie of it, since she'd acted like she thought it was about her. She'd wanted to keep the poem and Doolan said okay, not saying that he'd written it about Victoria Starner. So Doolan just stood there like a dummy until Annunciation called him a liar and kids started laughing and his ears got red and he got so mad he said *she* was the liar. She'd nearly yanked his ear off dragging him out of the room. Father Speer had shaken his head, then used his ruler on both of Doolan's outstretched palms.

Now it was the dancing. Poor Annie had the patience of a saint trying to teach Doolan to move to the music without clomping down on his partner's feet. It was called close dancing, but there was a heckuva space between Doolan and Annie, and you could put a third person between Pavoni and Louetta who weren't all that crazy about the idea.

Doolan went down the long outside flight of wooden steps, mailed his letter, and walked to Annie's.

"She can't see anyone," Mrs. Reardon told him. He thought she was going to say "especially you," but she didn't. She closed the door and he stood there trying to look cool in case Eddie was watching.

Doolan went back home. When his father was there, Doolan had slept on the living room sofa because the apartment had only two bedrooms. Now he had a room of his own. He did his push-ups and sit-ups, the linoleum cool against his bare back, took a bath in the rusty tub with the eagle-claw feet, and hopped into his father's bed.

Downstairs at Maloney's someone was trying to sing, and someone else was yelling. Doolan stuffed bits of tissue in his ears. As always, the first thing that popped into his head was the idea that the back door wasn't locked, though he remembered locking it. He never got up to check it again, but always wanted to.

His father had spent a lot of time sitting by the front window looking out at the traffic, but never said much. Doolan lay in the big double bed and tried to think of what his father would be thinking if he were lying here like he ought to be. Then he shut his eyes and imagined Saint Sebastian's catching fire during Sunday High Mass. He climbed to the choir loft where Victoria Starner was singing and grabbed her around the waist and swung to safety on one of the big lamps that hung on a gold chain from the vaulted ceiling. Victoria said she loved him forever.

Besides being the prettiest girl in the eighth grade and the only one who wore lipstick (not in school, but Doolan had seen her at her father's drugstore wearing red lipstick and rouge), Starner also had the best build. "Get a load of those knockers!" Kleinschmidt was always saying. Of course, Victoria Starner was Tom Duffy's girl. She paid no attention to Doolan or Pavoni, who were both crazy about her but who were only second string players on her boyfriend's football team, Doolan a defensive back and Pavoni an end.

Doolan wished it were summer. On Uncle Frank's farm they got up in the dark, walking with flashlights out to the barn, to milk the cows. Doolan loved to feel the cows' warm teats in his hands. He liked to hear the milk spraying tinny-sounding into the pail and the way the sound changed to a deeper bubbly one as the pail filled. He liked it so much he wondered if he ought to confess it, though he never did.

He liked his aunt and uncle too. Frank swore and chewed tobacco and let Doolan go off to the woods with the .22 rifle all by himself. Aunt Peg fried potato pancakes for Doolan, his favorite dish.

Sometimes Doolan caught himself wishing he was their son, and it made him feel bad. They weren't even Catholic. Uncle Frank drank whiskey. He slapped Aunt Peg on the bottom right in front of Doolan, or would give her a hug and kiss like it was the most natural thing in the world.

In the morning, Doolan was careful not to wake his mother. He ate a peanut butter sandwich and packed another one for his lunch.

He felt the other kids looking at him at Mass and knew they

knew all about it. He stood and knelt and prayed at the right times like it was any other day. He tried to see if Annie and Louetta were there, but couldn't get a good look at the girls' side of the aisle without turning his head, and knew that Annunciation and Petronilla would be watching to nail him for stepping out of line.

Doolan felt a bit better when the eighth grade filed into the classroom and he spotted Annie and Louetta. The girls kept their eyes down and he didn't try to talk to them. Doolan looked over to Pavoni. Tony was sitting straight up in his chair, staring dead ahead like he'd been frozen stiff. If Mr. Pavoni'd found out about the trouble, Tony's butt would be covered with welts. Sometimes it wasn't so bad not having a father around.

Anthony Flaherty, the class brain, a Mr. Peepers type who everybody knew was going to be a priest, went to the front of the room to do the daily reading from the Lives of the Saints.

"Our patron saint," Flaherty announced, "Saint Sebastian." He cleared his throat and looked around to make sure everybody was paying attention. " 'Saint Sebastian, an officer in the imperial household, encouraged his brothers in arms subjected to torments on account of their faith. Diocletian ordered him to be pierced with arrows. Sebastian, having escaped death, reappeared before the emperor and reproached him with his crimes. He was condemned to be flogged to death.' "

After that, it was Religion. Religion always came first, then Math, then English. Doolan suffered through each subject. Annunciation did not call on him and he did not raise his hand.

Every so often he peeked at Annie. She looked so sad it made him want to cry. That made him mad. Whenever he felt like crying, he got mad. He guessed he was weird that way. In his nightmares sometimes he told everybody how scared he got and how that made him so mad that he could kill somebody, anybody, even a nun or a priest. He got so scared then by what he'd said he would wet his pants right in front of the whole class. But he never told anybody how he felt or what he dreamed, so he guessed nobody knew how weird he was.

Annunciation started in on Geography. She told them about all the Catholic missions in all the different parts of the world.

Doolan looked past her at the big maps hanging from the rollers over the blackboard. The maps were so brown and cracked they looked like they'd been held over a fire until they almost burnt up, like martyrs, or like marines tortured by Japs. When he was a kid, Doolan used to dream of all the places he was going to go when he got big, China and Africa, the Amazon. He and Tony Pavoni had vowed to each other on pain of death that they'd go to Africa and be white hunters. That was in sixth grade; now, neither of them talked about it. Pavoni was going to Christ the King. His father said he'd get in less trouble there.

Doolan could hear the little kids outside screaming and yelling, playing red rover and dodge ball. Eighth graders were too old for recess.

Sister Mary Annunciation tapped the maps with a pointer: mission here, mission there. She hit kids with the pointer too. She'd have her back to them, then spin around and pick out somebody for talking and give him a good smack.

In the third grade, Doolan remembered, he had been stealing candy from the bowl Sister Benigna kept on her desk for spelling prizes. Doolan had never won a prize. There were jawbreakers in the bowl. Sister Benigna was out in the hall watching the other kids leave—Doolan had been kept after—when all of a sudden she said, "Dennis, let that candy alone." Doolan was scared. How could she know what he was doing when she wasn't even in the room? He thought then that nuns could see through walls like Superman.

At noon, Annunciation lined the class up along the wall before going to the lunchroom. Then she said, "Sister Mary Petronilla will walk you down today. Dennis Doolan, Anthony Pavoni, you stay behind."

Somebody said "Uh-oh," and kids laughed. Doolan's stomach sank, but he acted like it was nothing special. He stepped out of line and waited with Pavoni until the others had gone. When

Father Speer walked in, Doolan's stomach dropped right to his toes.

Father Speer was a big, heavy man, not fat though his face looked fat because it was red and puffy. Doolan thought the priest must always be mad about something, or else his Roman collar was too tight. Father Speer's hair was perfectly white, and in his long black cassock he looked like one of the saints on holy cards. He kept his hands folded behind his back, except when he hit you.

But Speer wasn't such a bad guy, all in all. He'd been all right to Doolan when he was serving early Mass. If Doolan showed up a couple of minutes late—it was hard getting up at six when he'd stayed up till midnight to talk to his mom—Speer wouldn't chew him out; he'd just say something like "A fine priest you'll make, Mr. Doolan, coming late to Mass." And lots of mornings after Mass the priest would tell Doolan to stop by the rectory kitchen where his housekeeper, Mrs. Kerns, would serve him breakfast.

The six-thirty service, a Low Mass on the side altar to Saint Joseph, was something most servers tried to dodge, but Doolan didn't mind it. He liked it, to tell the truth. The big church was cool and dim and the statues of the saints looked almost like real people in the candlelight, and he liked being the only server, just him and the priest on the altar, reciting the Latin and making the right moves at the right times. It was like being in a play. But Doolan knew the way he felt wasn't right because it wasn't religious. Probably all he was feeling was pride, which was a sin like most feelings were: pride in being up on the altar dressed in clean white vestments rather than kneeling in the pews with the black-habited nuns and the widows and a couple of old bachelors or drunks whispering their prayers into their folded hands.

"Are these the boys?" Speer asked Annunciation.

The nun nodded. Her chin looked as wrinkled as a walnut.

"Dennis Doolan," the priest said, and slowly shook his head.

"Yes, Father?"

"I'm disappointed in you, Dennis."

Why the priest should be disappointed in him since everybody at Saint Sebastian's knew he was trouble, Doolan didn't understand. "I know, Father."

"We should expel them," Annunciation said.

"I dint do nothing!" Pavoni cried out. "Honest to . . . Father, I dint."

Pavoni started to cry. If Tony got expelled, Mr. Pavoni would beat on him until there was nothing left.

"That's the truth, Father," Doolan said. "We were just learning to dance."

"Where?" Annunciation asked sharply.

"In the Reardons' basement, Father."

"And who was there?"

Doolan wished Annunciation would shut her trap. He'd like to see her scream and melt like the witch in "Wizard of Oz." "Father, it was just Tony and me. And the girls."

"Who was down there with you?" the nun asked. "To chaperone?"

"Mrs. Reardon was there, Father."

Father Speer sighed. "Could she see you, Dennis?"

"Was she in the basement with you at the time? All the time?" Annunciation asked. "Don't lie to me. I know what went on down there."

"She was upstairs, Father, but all we did was practice dancing."

"Why?" Father Speer asked, looking right at Doolan.

" 'Cause I don't know how. Tony and me, we don't have any sisters to teach us. We're gonna have to go to dances and we don't know how to dance."

"Louetta Shoemacker and the Reardon girl, Father," Annunciation said. "I called them in yesterday. I told them I knew what was going on down there . . ."

"You've got a dirty mind!" Doolan cried, his face hot.

Annunciation slapped Doolan's cheek, but he was pulling away and there was little sting to it. He stepped back, knotting up his fists.

"Stop this!" Speer said. "Put down your hands, Dennis."

"Father, all I . . ."

"And speak when you're spoken to."

"He has to be expelled," Annunciation said.

"Father, I'm telling the truth!" Tears came to Doolan's eyes; he could not keep them back. "She wasn't there. Nothing happened. That's the truth."

Annunciation turned to her desk and picked up the pointer.

"You hit me," Doolan said, "and my dad's gonna call the cops on you."

"Sister," Speer said.

Annunciation lay down the pointer. Her face was as white as paste.

"Dennis," the priest said. "This is a very serious matter."

"The C.Y.O. has dances," Doolan said. "Christ the King has dances."

"You boys go home now," Speer said.

"Am I gonna be expelled?" Pavoni didn't look up when he spoke.

"I'll see you tomorrow after Mass." The priest turned away from them. "Sister, please bring the girls to see me."

The next day Doolan and Pavoni waited in the rectory kitchen. Mrs. Kerns didn't offer them anything to eat.

Pavoni was called in first. Doolan stood with his back to a wall, arms crossed over his chest and hands tucked into his armpits.

When his turn came, he walked slowly down the purple-carpeted hall. He expected to see Tony, but didn't. He guessed Pavoni must have been sent out the front way, so he couldn't warn Doolan about what was coming. Like in the movies when the Japs kept the captured marines from talking to each other.

Speer was sitting behind a big black desk. He told Doolan to sit. The straight-backed wooden chair faced the desk. Father Speer looked steadily at Doolan, but said nothing. A grandfather clock beside a wall of books ticked like a bomb.

"Well, Dennis, did you learn how to dance?"

Doolan thought the priest might be trying to joke with him, but he wasn't in the mood. It felt like there were wires inside him pulled tight; it was the way he felt when he had to fight a guy.

"I asked you a question, Dennis."

"I'm not so good yet, Father, but I'll keep practicing."

"A priest doesn't have to know how to dance, but he has to be able to tell the truth."

"I'm doing that, Father."

"You are."

Doolan didn't know if it was a question or not. "I'm not going to be a priest, anyway."

"And when did you change your mind about that?"

"I never said I was, Father."

"Dennis, you're a smart boy. You've been in some trouble, but everybody gets into trouble somewhere along the way."

Some of the babushkas Doolan's mother talked with after Sunday Mass gossiped about the pastor having been a wild young man. He'd had to leave the seminary once, they said. The women leaned close when they talked, then laughed and pulled back, making little o's of their mouths. When Speer came up to them, they got shy and quiet, like he was the pope himself.

"I don't want to be a priest," Doolan said. He wanted to say he'd never wanted to be one, but that would be a lie; for a year or so, when he dropped the white hunter idea, he'd thought it wouldn't be so bad being head of a church and telling the nuns what to do.

Speer nodded. "No, you don't want to be a priest, do you."

All of a sudden Doolan felt really sad, and wished that he and the priest were talking to each other in Latin. He thought it was weird of him to wish that.

"Did you tell the others what to say?"

"No, Father."

"When a boy gets your age, Dennis, it's hard for him to know what to do." Speer hunched forward over the black desk. Behind him on the wall was a framed picture of the Sacred Heart. Jesus opened up his chest and pointed to a red heart giving off a bright light like it was something really powerful, like kryptonite. "It gets hard for him to think of his faith. The world seems exciting and the church seems dull." After they listened to the clock tick for a time, Speer asked, "Isn't that true?"

"I guess so, Father."

"You have to make choices in this life, Dennis. If you make the wrong ones, you'll pay for them the rest of your life."

Doolan nodded.

"You're certain you've told me the truth?"

"Yes, Father."

The priest looked at a gold wristwatch. The parishioners said Speer came from a rich family, and Doolan guessed he did because every other year the priest got a new set of wheels, always a big Chrysler. He was driving a '58 Imperial now, a two-door black hardtop with whitewalls and loads of chrome. Doolan checked it out in the church lot every chance he got. It had a big V-8 with a four-barrel carburetor and power steering and Torqueflite transmission. Doolan bet it could go like hell.

"I'm going to let the other children off this time, but I have to suspend you. For three days. Do you know why?"

"No, Father, I don't."

"Dennis?" Speer stood. He looked awfully big in the black cassock with his broad red face and white hair. "You should never speak to a nun as you did. Do you realize what a nun is?"

"She teaches religion."

"A nun is the bride of Christ."

Doolan nodded.

"That's all, Dennis."

Doolan hesitated in the carpeted hall, wondering if he should use the front or back door.

"Is there something you want to say?"

He guessed the priest thought he ought to say thank you or I'm sorry. "No, Father." He went out the front door.

When he left the apartment the next morning, his mother was still sleeping. He hadn't told her of his suspension; she had enough to worry about. Three whole days of freedom ahead of him, Doolan stood at the top of the long flight of stairs above the parking lot for Maloney's Bar & Grill. His father had tended bar for Maloney; Doolan used to stop in after school and his father would set him up an orange soda and give him a dime to play shuffleboard. "If you're smart," his father said, "you won't ever get married. You listen to the priests. They got it knocked, those boys."

The bells were ringing for eight o'clock Mass at Saint Sebastian's. The sky looked big and the air felt clean, like it did just after Doolan made a good confession and came out of church, his penance said, feeling fresh and new. It wasn't quite the same feeling now. He felt lonely, but not really sad; maybe not lonely exactly, just alone.

If he never went to church again, he knew what he'd be: fallen away. His father had been fallen away. If you stayed fallen away, you were damned. Your soul burnt in fires hotter than the one in the school furnace. He'd watched Mr. Karavas empty the big wastebaskets into the furnace. All the messed-up assignments and secret notes and Kleinschmidt's dirty drawings went into the fire and were burnt up. Hell was like that, except you never got freed by being burnt up. You just kept burning.

At Dotty Condon's party, Doolan and Pavoni in pink shirts and pegged charcoal pants stood by the record player. "We're the DeeJays," they told the girls who tried to get them out to the center of the basement where couples were dancing. Pavoni was nuts about the Platters and kept playing "Only You" and "My Prayer." Every so often Doolan put on Fats Domino or Elvis.

Kleinschmidt prowled the edge of the dance floor, making big eyes and grabbing at his heart at the way some guy was holding a girl.

Dotty's mom and dad had been downstairs, but after a while got bored or embarrassed and went up. Kleinschmidt turned out the overhead light and two of the three lamps. Duffy and Starner were having a fight, it looked like, and she was sitting in a corner. Her pink sweater was tight and Pavoni said he was going to ask her to dance before the party was over. Doolan knew he wouldn't. None of the guys made a move on Starner because they were scared she'd say no and the other guys would laugh. Duffy was dancing with lots of girls. He'd danced with Annie four times, holding her really close and dipping her at the end of the song. She was wearing a lavender dress Doolan had never seen before.

Kleinschmidt came over. "It's the Big Bopper!" He crouched and waggled his legs back and forth. He had some wine outside and wanted Doolan and Pavoni to come out and try it. Doolan told him to drop dead. Kleinschmidt pulled something from his pocket. "Fish-skins," he whispered. He pushed them at Pavoni. "Whyn't you see if you can get Louetta to come outside." Pavoni gave him a shove. Kleinschmidt said watch it or he'd get his brother. He grinned and jerked his head at Annie being steered around by Tom Duffy. "Maybe I'll see if Duffy wants these."

Doolan spun Kleinschmidt around and kicked him in the butt, hard. Pavoni took a kick at him too. "I'll get my brothers," he said. "We'll kick your ass and your brother's ass too."

"Hardeharhar," Kleinschmidt said. "Tell me another one, yo-yo." He glared at the two of them, but moved away.

Pavoni laughed. "We're big stuff now. We're freshmen."

"Tough guys," Doolan said.

"Bad asses." Pavoni punched Doolan on the arm and Doolan punched him back. They laughed again. Doolan would miss Pavoni. Eli Whitney was a rival of Christ the King and Doolan didn't like thinking that sometime he'd have to nail Pavoni coming out for a pass.

Doolan put on "Wake Up Little Susie." It was fast and half the guys let go of their partners and left the floor. They didn't know how to fast dance either. A few couples did the chicken or a jitterbug. Duffy, who had sisters good enough to be on "Bandstand," kept Annie with him and started in on the Bop.

The next record was Pavoni's. He went for Little Anthony and the Imperials, "Tears on My Pillow." When Annie swung by, she looked over Duffy's shoulder and mouthed "Break in. Please."

"What's she trying to tell us?" Pavoni wanted to know.

Doolan tapped Duffy on the shoulder. "My turn."

Duffy didn't even look at him. "Get lost."

"You think I'm kidding!" Doolan said. He grabbed Duffy's sweater, yanking it out of shape. Duffy spun around, but Annie got in between them. She took Doolan's fists and put his arms around her and then they were moving off to the slow big swings of the music.

"Lead with your left," Annie whispered.

Doolan did his best. He knew everybody was watching them, but told himself he couldn't care less.

"Thanks," Annie said. "I can't stand that creep."

"Duffy?" Tom Duffy looked like Tab Hunter and Doolan thought that all the girls were crazy about him.

"He's got bad breath."

Doolan laughed. He stopped when Annie moved so close to him he could feel the bumps of her chest. When the song ended, she didn't let go of his hand, so he stood beside her waiting for something to happen. If Duffy started anything, Doolan would kick him in the family jewels first thing.

Pavoni played "Earth Angel" and Doolan and Annie took up where they'd left off. Doolan let his right hand slide down to the small of Annie's back. He was surprised at how warm she felt, and how easily they moved together.

"How'd you do on your grade card?" Annie asked.

"All D's."

"I thought you were getting a B in Geography."

"And in Math. That's the way the ball bounces."

"Sister Annunciation!" Annie hissed. "I hate her, that prune."

Doolan pressed his hand against Annie's back and she put her whole body right up against him. He thought he would faint. Sweat ran into his eyes. Annie's cheek was against his and he pulled back his head so he wouldn't sweat on her.

They stayed together for three more dances, all Platters tunes, before Annie said she had to go. Without giving himself a chance to get nervous, Doolan said he could walk her home. "If that's okay with you. I mean, if nobody's picking you up or anything."

Outside, he didn't try to hold her hand. They walked real slow and Annie kind of swayed like she was still dancing and every so often they bumped together.

"My folks aren't mad at you."

"They're not?" Doolan said.

"I told them what you did. You did the right thing. I just *hate* that nun!"

"Me too," Doolan said.

The Reardons' porch light was on. Doolan and Annie stopped by a tree in front of her house. "You're going to Whitney, aren't you?"

Doolan nodded, looking at his feet.

"Well," Annie said. "We'll still live close, you know."

"Sure." When he looked up, Annie was smiling. He reached out and held her by the shoulders and leaned forward and kissed her on the lips. She kissed him back. Her hands gave his shoulders a squeeze before she moved away. Doolan stuck his hands in his armpits. "I'll call you. That okay?"

"I want you to," Annie said. She walked up the steps onto the porch and gave him a little wave. Beneath the yellow light in the lavender dress, she looked beautiful. He stood on the walk not knowing what to do. Then she went in.

Doolan walked up the middle of the street, whistling and kicking a beer can. He had kissed a girl, a girl he'd thought was his friend, or was only his friend. He guessed now he had a girl. He would write to her over the summer and maybe she'd want him to go to dances with her at Christ the King; maybe she'd go to one with him at Eli Whitney and they'd all see that he had his own girl.

He felt so happy. He knew he ought to feel bad. Maybe that was how you felt at first when you were fallen away. He thought of Speer in his black cassock behind the black desk. Maybe later you found out you had to pay for all those times you thought you were happy.

Still, Doolan felt happy. He gave the can a terrific kick, flipping it into the air to land, clattering away. As long as he was damned, he'd be a damned fool not to enjoy it.

Comedy of Eros

In the late summer of that year I lived in an apartment on the West Side that looked out over Columbus Avenue. On the street there were yellow cabs and gassy busses and platoons of cyclists with whistles in their mouths and roller skaters along the curb. They streamed toward midtown where business towers stood like fortresses. Dust, stirred by the traffic, rose and fell. Secretaries and receptionists and editorial assistants marched past on Adidas and Nikes, their office heels stowed in nylon backpacks.

It was a bad time. Billie was gone and so was the French girl. Billie had taken a holiday in Spain and Sabine was off men since her operation. My ex was dating one of my colleagues, a bald WASP, a turncoat who taught a course in the philosophy of feminism.

I spent mornings drinking coffee and smoking Luckies, re-reading Hemingway and trying to believe that in time my present desolation would ease into that lyrical sense of loss I found in Papa's *A Farewell to Arms.* Afternoons, I jogged in Central Park, passing the bench homesteaders and bag ladies and stoned Rasta-farians and old Hebrew widows leashed to tiny white puffs of dogs. Around the reservoir I chased the silky inverted heart shape of a female tail. The gravel path was flanked by green leafy branches and chain link fencing, and gulls sailed out over the water. Heavy with sweaty flesh, I made my way. A voice in my mind, like the narrator on the old *Victory at Sea* television show, summed up my state: "That summer he was hard pressed, morale was low, and his flagging campaign took on the look of a strategic retreat." I ran on, my face red, my heart gone purple with what I feared was permanent pain.

As usual, I was on the rebound. For a while I'd been seeing one of my students, a fellatio major, then had taken up with Jill whom I found in the *New York Review of Books* personals: *DWF. Slim, stunning, brainy, unfulfilled, adventurous. Seeks SWM. Object: fun.* As it turned out Jill's idea of fun was torturing men. She would trick herself out in leather and black net hose and claim a headache when I touched her, arrange a meeting and not show up, then come to my place at three in the morning, no apologies, but breathy and eager, dying for it. She was a Rubik's Cube of neuroses. We were miserable together; we called it *passion.*

Evenings, alone, I tried to read as people under my window sang and laughed and hailed taxis. There was traffic all night; after the cabs came supply trucks for Sushi bars and Mexican cantinas and the sidewalk cafes with authentic espresso and seasonal spritzers. Toward morning garbage trucks nosed along the curb behind squads of chattering, can-banging blacks.

When Jill had broken it off for good, it hurt, yet I felt immediate relief. My whole place to myself again, and my time. Hallelujah! Three days later I was in a panic, bouncing off walls and drinking from the bottle. I dialed Jill's number like a junkie calling his source. She used her answering device as a screen; I'd been with her when she did it to others. I knew she was hiding behind her taped greeting, "Hi! So glad you called!", enjoying my begging, and I knew she knew I knew. I began ringing her up in the middle of the night, stuporous with booze and Valium, to deposit despicable, sick messages on her tape. Then in the grip of a morning hangover I'd call again to leave a message saying not to listen to my other messages. Maybe she'd netted a better catch with a new ad; whatever, she never returned my calls. Only Warren, my ex-chairman, called. He left messages on my Panasonic Easa-Phone, extolling the delights of married life and reporting on his progress in staying on the wagon. I couldn't bring myself to call him back. He'd be ashamed of me. Was I a man or a mouse? Was I pussy-whipped or what? I felt exhausted, shell-shocked. I couldn't stand my own company. I needed to be saved.

In August, near the end of the month, Claire appeared. She wore a white dress belted with a braided cord of cerulean blue. She looked the slightest bit hippy, charming in a baby-fat way, and oddly maternal. Her black hair tumbled in curls. Amethyst dots studded her ears. I was at her office to press my suit with an editor who'd shown interest in *Lost Causes,* my study of key defeats in military history. I treated Crassus at the battle of Carrhae, Charles XII of Sweden at Poltava, and the serial disaster of Ambrose Burnside's entire career. I'd punched up a new closing chapter on Westmoreland in Vietnam which I hoped would make the manuscript more relevant, meaning commercial. When Claire asked my name, her voice was a breathy little whisper, yet her chin showed independence. She had graceful, long-fingered hands and a swan's neck. Love dropped its brick on my graying head.

After the young editor in jeans and denim shirt (I'd chosen to wear a three-piece suit) had given me a smile, his regrets, and directions to the exit, Claire saw me to the elevator. Her look seemed to offer solace. When I took her hand she seemed pleased, yet showed no disappointment when I let it go. The elevator door closed twice on my foot before I got up the nerve to ask if I could call her. She hesitated, then nodded. I plucked my pen from my shirt pocket. She gave me her name, and, when I asked for her number, said, "I'm in the book."

"Of course." It was another rejection, and I let the doors slide shut.

But she was in the book after all, and I called her all that afternoon and evening, seven times, but there was no answer until six-forty. Keeping my voice as casual as possible, my hands trembling, I suggested that she might like to go hear the Harlem Jazz Kings at the Ginger Man, if she were free, if she had nothing on. "I'll meet you there," she said.

I expected her to call back and say something had come up. She was sorry, but. I shaved, showered, and the phone rang as I was blow-drying my thinning hair. It was Warren. The volume was up on my answering machine and he sounded as though he spoke through a bullhorn.

"Cohen on the telephone," he said. "Yis, gone is der golden days of vaudeville. But listen up, numb-nuts, here's a titbit from papa Freud might grab you. In evolution the olfactory sense was separated from the human sex drive, giving rise to visual excitations; you know, like my own Wan Wai's gorgeous gams. 'So,' quoting here, 'a moment came when the need for genital satisfaction no longer made its appearance like a guest who drops in suddenly, and after his departure, is heard of no more for a long time'—Germanic awkwardness, that construction—'but instead took up its quarters as a permanent lodger.' Well put, huh? So the male of our species is in perpetual rut."

He ran out of tape time and hung up. I brushed my hair and opened a beer. For courage. Just before the battle, mother. Warren called back. "So here we are—in *Civilization and Its Discontents*, Norton paperback, book four, page forty-six, footnote one: 'The diminution of the olfactory stimuli seems in itself to be a consequence of man's raising himself from the ground, of his assumption of an upright gait; this made his genitals, which were previously concealed, visible and in need of protection.' The family jewels on public display, ay? We get nailed where it hurts the worst. 'And,' Freud again, 'so provoked feelings of shame in him.' There you go in a nutshell. New paragraph. 'The fateful process of civilization would thus have set in with man's adoption of an erect posture.' No wonder we need to get laid. Adios."

Claire kept her word. I couldn't believe my good luck. We sat at a tiny table too close to the saxophone. She wore a white blouse, a full blue skirt, and a white hibiscus in her hair. The top two buttons of her blouse were open to provide—forgive me, father, for I have seen—a glimpse of white bra. She drank Chablis. Between numbers, we told each other all about ourselves, meaning those items of experience we thought put us in a favorable light. I explained how painful my divorce had been. She'd grown up in Connecticut, she said, had gone to a little Episcopal college in Illinois, was twenty-four, and wanted to be an editor. To my surprise, we closed the place. We strolled along Central Park West. Alert for muggers, I listened to her count the beads of her heartbreaks: abandoned by the college boy she'd been engaged to, pursued by a married editor who later drank Lysol, hurt by her father's divorcing her mother. She saw a woman therapist now, and hoped eventually to have a place in New Hampshire, an herb garden, pets, and cross-country skiing each winter. As a historian, I told her, I too was dismayed by the lack of faith our age suffered from. Her contacts fouled by grit, she tilted back her head to squeeze artificial tears in her eyes. She was stacked, no doubt about it. When I invited her to my apartment, she smiled and said, "Thanks anyway." I calculated how much her perfect teeth must have cost her father. At twenty-four, she looked alive and bright as her white hibiscus. I was two months shy of the four-oh, that one-way ticket from sin city to Sun City, and my heart greeted each new day with incipient fear. I tried to hold her hand, but she neatly slipped free.

During the next weeks, we went to Shakespeare in the park, *The Comedy of Errors,* saw *Amadeus* twice, arguing a bit when I sided with Salieri, heard Angela Bofil sing "Over the moon and under the stars" under the stars on a blanket on an East River pier, and ate turnip greens and chitlins at the Pink Teacup in the Village. "This is wonderful," I told her. "I've never had so much fun. It's like a honeymoon, almost."

"Almost," she said.

I went with her to sessions of consciousness raising. Her guru, a midget the color of curry, with white flowers in his tangled black hair and wearing a saffron robe, sat cross-legged on a dais and urged us in a voice like a sitar to "bleez, geev eet up."

I raised my hand to ask, "If man were meant to live within his limits, why was the extension cord invented?"

Claire tugged at my sleeve. The guru focused on a point directly above my unbowed head. "You are all koh-meed-yens. I am beg of you. Geev eet up. Bleez."

What "eet" was I wasn't sure but I wanted to believe that, like Claire, I could believe. I ate vegetables with her rather than animals, drank herbal tea, and learned to chant a mantra.

She began spending evenings at my place, yet consistently refused to go beyond the heavy necking I'd thought consigned to the dark ages of my youth. Still, I was happy with her. Her strict limits made me feel young. Everything old is new again. It amazed me. But that's love for you.

We took long walks along the nightly carnival of Columbus Avenue. I felt proud to have her with me, hand in hand now. She looked so fresh, a talisman against the surrounding corruption.

One night she told me how she dreamed of white birches, and asked what I thought that meant. Flattered, I said romance. "You're a romantic."

"True," she said, "and I hope to die one."

I gave her my weathered cynic's grin. "Your chances of that are good. Romance is a terminal disease." She laughed. She seemed to know that where she was concerned I was a sheep in wolf's clothing.

I took to calling her my white birch, crooning the words in the warm hollow of her collarbone as we embraced in the foyer of her apartment building. In her tiny whisper she confided that as a young girl on her parents' farm she had climbed a white birch. Riding the swaying branches, she had come for the first time. "So that's what birches mean," I cried. I held her in my arms and we laughed. Just like in the movies. Why not? Once again I saw my life in technicolor with a soaring score, heavy on strings. Yet my body felt a constant, loaded ache. I implored her to sleep with me. She refused. I told her I admired her scruples, but really, she couldn't limit her sex life to trees. What I had in mind was no one-night stand. Didn't she think she was making too big a thing out of natural affection between adults? I was the one making too much of it, she said. "Really, there are higher things."

"Hell," I snapped, "I know that." But I couldn't stay angry with her. Her face shone with such a clear light. Claire de Lune, free and Claire, and my heart sang in her presence. Yes, I succumbed to all the clichés of young love. I felt happy, even lucky, to be this dizzy in the head and sick to the stomach, to have such a fierce case of what in the age of zits and Roman hands we'd called blue balls.

She had flaws, of course. I wasn't blind. Besides virginity, she had a penchant for pop psych and gauzy theosophy. Dog-eared paperbacks on *Our Inner Life* and *The Past in Your Present* littered her room. "Do you think we knew each other in a former life?" she wondered.

"Do we in this one?" I asked.

And despite, or because of, working in publishing, she couldn't spell. Childish errors made her impromptu notes a source of amusement to me, albeit a bit of an embarrassment as well, since the quality of the chosen woman reflects on that of the man. "Sweat dreams," she'd write, letting me know she cared for me "alot."

But these seemed minor flaws in the light of her presence. I bought her a pearl necklace, and gold bracelets for wrist and ankle. We cooked meals at my place and played Parcheesi. Her stereo was on the fritz so she brought her albums over to play on mine, the Beatles, Joan Collins, Phoebe Snow. I was pleased she didn't go for hard rock; it seemed to lessen the gap between our ages. We cuddled on the couch, sipping gin fizzes, listening in the dark to taxi horns and Cat Stevens. Morning has broken like the first morning. I truly believed it had.

I began picturing us in an A-frame of natural wood and clear glass set among shade trees in New Hampshire. Brisk fall days flooded our lives with light. Claire and a fireplace radiated warmth. Black dog slumbered on the hearth and Snow, a white cat, sat watching in a window. Claire and I felt one another's presence as a daily gift, not a duty or a burden. There were no sulks, no nights spent with one of us exiled to the sofa, no bogging down in simple decisions made difficult by the need to appease two separate wills. No biological alarm ticking away in her would sound off *baby baby baby* to transform the young career woman into a mama and disrupt our harmony. Renewed by her love, I would suffer no boredom with home-front comforts, nor itch for the city's sexual skirmishes. Because my first marriage had been wiped out in such a no man's land did not mean a second foray was doomed to fail. It's those who don't know history who are condemned to repeat it; I knew my life's history by heart.

But she wasn't mine, not yet. She had her own place, her own friends, her own interests. Certain things about her—all right, it was the sex—made her seem archaic and selfish, even retarded. Such dark feelings made me feel bad about myself. Although I said I loved her, some part of me murmured that if I really loved her I wouldn't keep pushing her. Maybe I wasn't capable of real love. Maybe I was just, as she said, infatuated.

I lied to her as a matter of course. My occasional whore, for instance. A man dealing with a woman learns early on to lie if he hopes to keep her around a while. When Claire excitedly told me of her plans to spend the weekend at East Hampton at a girl friend's place, I said without blinking that I didn't mind, even as the continuing documentary of my life stated: "It was all very fine that summer until the rich came in, like little fish feeding off a hooked shark. The rich can ruin many things for many people."

"Sure," I said, "go." Hippy, busty, Claire would be a knockout in a swim suit, and although I'd not seen her I knew that the girl friend would look great too. The rich can afford to appear beautiful even when they're not. I said, "Why should I mind?"

We'd given each other keys to our places, as an act of faith, I suppose. As soon as Claire was off to the beach, I went through her things. It didn't seem shabby. I saw it as further proof of how nuts I was about her. Possessed by love, the documentary intoned, a film close-up of my hand in her underwear drawer, possessed by love, he broke all the rules. Her diary entries were mainly questions. Such as: *Are older men better?* At what? I wondered, or than what? The date of the entry, that past Sunday, meant she'd written it the day after a very heavy petting session, dry-fucking we used to call it, on my sofa. So she had been moved to new insights, or questions at least. It did bother me some that she put it as a question. Why not a conclusion? Yet most of her entries were questions: *What do I really want in my life? Is the city really good for me?* I kept forgetting how young she was. She was still at that age when one takes the asking of big questions as a sign of one's fundamental seriousness, not just muddle-headedness. *Older* men? Was I that old? Would she take to calling me Papa? Did she think it was only the infirmity of my years that kept me from ravishing her?

When she returned from her weekend, she didn't want to see me. "I look awful," she said on the phone.

"I don't care," I told her, "I'm coming."

She had lain out in the sun too long. Her pink face was puffy. She wore a man's white shirt many sizes too big for her—her father's?—and her legs glistened with Solarcaine. Touching her was out of the question. I brought her washcloths soaked in tea for her blazing forehead, and repeatedly told her I loved her. She would only smile and twitch her head, shaking off my words.

Many times, especially toward the ends of our fevered evenings together, I would urge upon her the fact of my love. I did love her. I had to. It drove me into a rage that she refused to admit the reality of my feeling. For weeks she hadn't said anything about what she felt for me, then admitted she was afraid to love me. Now she said she was afraid she loved me. I didn't argue with her. I accepted it. And I felt that all that was needed to make my love for her a fact beyond doubt was for her to agree to it. History is not the only agreed-upon fable, and what sane man doubts history's reality? If Claire would admit my half, our love would be complete, a regained wholeness to which our physical union would give tangible form.

But she claimed that all I felt for her was passion.

"No," I said, "I love you."

"Just the other day I was reading how real love is not possessive."

"Those cockamamie psych books! I'm telling you I love you."

She gave me a faint smile. "You don't even know me."

"Well, it's not for lack of trying."

"Oh not that way, I mean really."

"I don't have to know you to know that I love you."

"Oh yes," she said, "you do." She looked so calm and certain in these exchanges. How is it that a young woman who can't spell can seem to possess age-old wisdom while well-schooled men bumble through life like boys?

At the end of one such evening, I pitched *Our Inner Life* at her head, screaming, "I don't love you? You cunt! I idolize you!" She turned me out and refused to speak to me for three days. God knows how long my exile might have gone on if I hadn't persevered in setting things to rights. She had no machine for me to leave messages on, so I hand-delivered letters to her building, apologizing at length and abasing myself with pleas for permission to return to her good graces. I tried to take the sting, for me, out of these peace entreaties by signing them R. Dent Voryu, Fook Kong Sori, and Attila the Honey. In case she wasn't opening my letters, I had expensive bouquets delivered to her at the office.

Claire didn't write, didn't call. Warren called, of course.

"So here you go, Bucko," his recorded voice yapped. "We can do this in the fall at the faculty follies. To the tune of 'The Legend of Davey Crockett.'" He hummed a bar, announced "The Ballad of Andy Scruder," and sang in his smokey voice:

> Born in the Village in thirty-three,
> Freed of conventional morality,
> Found him a lass, professed her the one,
> To enroll in his course in the history of fun—
> Andy, Andy Scruder,
> Three times before he was done.

"More later," he said. And there was.

> Chaired his department with an iron hand,
> Ran things as smoothly as a prostate gland,
> Cleared off his desk, a conference at one,
> Two and three went by, my how the time did run—
> Andy, Andy Scruder,
> Three times, etc., etc.

"So get in touch, will you?"

I called him back later that night. "Where the hell you been?" he roared. "How about a boys night out, a pub crawl, a hell-raiser, a howl at the moon?" I told him I wasn't up to it. "So what are you up to these days?"

"Not much," I said.

"Me neither. I'm having a run of bad luck."

"How's that?"

"Ah, me and the little woman, Bucko, we ain't seeing eye to eye; of course she's a lot shorter than me. But we'll work it out, or in, something."

I said I was having a little female trouble myself.

"Buck up," Warren said. "Remember your Theocritus, Sonny: 'There is hope for the living, but none for the dead.' So long."

The letters and flowers worked, of course. There might be age-old wisdom in Claire's pretty head, or in her blood, but her heart was still that of the little girl delighted to get presents. She took me back, and I was happy. I certainly acted happy. Yet it nettled me that I had to beg.

In the grip of love, that vague malais, you may be prompted to large gestures of generosity, even to the sharing of your daily life; yet at the same time some part of you wonders just how much a man ought to put up with for a woman's sake, and questions at what point do you become a patsy, although this may be judged selfishness. And you can't go on forever being a patsy—from the Italian, *pazzo,* meaning madman—but at some point have to make a stand.

So one evening at my place, I got a couple of stiff drinks into her, gin and tonic heavy on gin, the ice cubes clinking against the glasses like plinked piano keys, minor notes to the night's orchestration, and served up spaghetti with a spicy sauce and kept filling our stemmed glasses with Chianti. We offered toasts to health and happiness. I held her eyes with mine across the flickering flames of the beeswax candles. "God, you look beautiful," I told her, "so lovely it makes me want to weep."

"Oh," she said, and glanced away, and said it again, "Oh." True romance stuff, but let's face it: a cliché only gets to be a cliché because it actually happens countless times.

After I'd cleared the dishes, and we'd each had a thimble's worth of aquavit, we sat on the sofa and hugged and kissed as Cat Stevens sang pure praise to the morning and, despite her muted protests, I began to go for two out of three falls.

Excited as I was, seriously engaged in action, it struck me as odd that I also seemed to be observing myself from a distance. The aquavit perhaps. *Victory at Sea* told the story: "Having trouble with the straps of the formidable brassiere, he finally succeeded in freeing the hooks. There was a brief struggle then as he attempted to clear the white mountains entirely, but soon he was successful in this as well. Now the theatre of operations shifted to the white V-shaped island of panties, and he concentrated all his forces to eliminating them as the final obstacle to penetration."

Andy Scruder.

And afterwards, he, I, lay on my back on the floor with her still on the sofa above me. Her hand trailed down so that her fingertips lightly touched the curling hair on my chest. "You look so somber."

I shrugged.

"I know," she said, the informed *Cosmo* reader, "it's post-coital tristesse, isn't it?"

"With me, sweetie," I said, "it's post-natal tristesse." I put my arm over my eyes so I wouldn't have to look at her.

At the crucial moment, at that point at which she still could have said no and made me listen, she had sighed and, a bit peevishly I thought, said, "Oh all right." She'd sat up on the sofa, naked but for necklace and sandals, to fumble in her purse —"Let me take out my eyes"—and stowed her contacts in a tiny white case. "There," she said, businesslike, and returned to me, although by now I was less than eager, even diminished. Now that I knew I could have her, it didn't seem so important. Yet it went deeper than that. I felt freshly tainted by guilt. As she'd been seeing to her eyes, I couldn't help but note in the light from the hall that her skin was a splotchy red from her recent sunburn, her shoulders were peeling, her flesh was slightly puffy, even doughy, and her breasts sagged. At thirty she'd be in woeful shape. Jaded, the documentary intoned, he turned his back on life's simple pleasures in a fruitless search for exotic delights. And to make things worse, I was aware that just beneath my enduring animal excitement I was experiencing a definite sense of release, even freedom perhaps, in recognizing the ordinariness of her body. So this is what all the fuss is about! Where was that magic, that power I'd so feared? Just another little joke on man, the god in ruins, the thinking reed, the only animal that blushes, or needs to.

And now, after the act, I saw no magic at all. She'd been passive; at best, patient. That transcendent calm I'd envied appeared now to be nothing more than bovine stupor. It all fell into place —her composure, her whispers and giggles, her girlish enjoyment of daily routine, her misspellings. She was a nitwit. I should give up my freedom for this?

"You okay?" I asked. She said she was fine. "But you didn't," I said, "you know, did you?" She said it was different with her, she didn't have to, not every time.

Then she asked, "Do you always tell me the truth?"

"Yes and no," I said.

"Are you happy now?"

"Why shouldn't I be? Let's not talk it to death, all right?"

"All right," she said, "but are we close?"

"What?"

"We close?"

"Sure," I said, "*huis clos,*" and noted it for Warren. So I was a bastard, I thought, so who wasn't? Then it hit me, jackknifing me into a sitting position. "Every time?" I squawked. "You don't have to, *every time?* What's this every time? I thought this was your first." She shook her head, coyly. "Second?" I asked. Another shake. "All right, third, fourth? What is this, twenty questions?"

"Don't," she said, sounding hurt, "it's not funny."

"It sure as hell isn't!" She put a hand on my chest to press me back onto the floor. I didn't resist. I wished she could have pushed me right down through it to the basement with the rest of the junk.

She slid from the sofa to lie beside me, using my arm as her pillow. "I feel I can tell you," she said in her little voice. "It was right after my dad left home. I'd just come to the city and felt so lost here." Then she began ticking them off—an artist, a waiter, an actor, her first boss, an ad man, a cousin, well third cousin, two musicians she'd roomed with, the super at her building. Holy cow, I thought, no wonder she's into former lives. I stopped her when she'd listed enough men to field a football team, with depth on the bench.

"See?" she said, "I came to see it was a dead end. My therapist says I was punishing myself, like it was all my fault what happened at home. I think she's probably right, don't you?"

I made some kind of animal noise. Whatever it was, she seemed to take it as proof of my mature understanding and acceptance. Weren't older men better? I couldn't meet her eyes. I glanced sidelong at her graceful neck, its span about that of my two hands.

"But that was over a year ago," she said. She hadn't seen any of them since. She'd made up her mind to start all over, to save herself for someone special. "Like you," she said. And now she was glad she had.

"A born-again virgin," I said, grinning like a skull. The documentary sounded loud and clear: "Discovering he'd been betrayed, he turned bitter. He waged a scorched earth campaign. He granted no quarter."

"What does it matter," I said, "aren't we both adults?"

She gave me a little squeeze: "I hoped you'd be this way."

If I was heartless it was because I felt she'd cut the heart right out of me. I felt, I guess, like Columbus might have if, landing on what he expected to be the fresh, green breast of the new world, he'd stumbled onto tract after tract of V.A. housing. So I got up and took milady, this Levittown of sexual experience, by the hand and led her down the hall to the bedroom where I kept her at it most of the night; for a man near forty, no mean feat. A few times she tried to call a halt to it, and once cried, "That hurts!" but I was beyond caring. I kept at it even when I tasted the tears on her face. Finished, I collapsed on the bed beside, but not touching, her. The air conditioner droned, dripping. "Like Burnside before him," the documentary went on, muted and slow as if its generating power were running low, "he proved to be a fool. In campaign after campaign he managed to snatch defeat from the jaws of victory." The voice ran down into a blubbery incoherence and I slept the sleep of the just laid.

When I woke, the sheets smelled of her but she was gone. There was a note on my night stand:

> I thought you were diffrent, that you'd understand. I guess I was wrong. You don't have to feel obiligated. This is all just a comedy of erros. I should have known better. Maybe now I'll learn.

Erros, that was her style. How could I know what she meant when she couldn't spell it out? I called her at work and was told she'd called in sick. I tried her place, but got no answer. One thing I didn't need was to get sucked into a moral court-martial stacked to prove me guilty. Born-again virgin might have been too harsh, but it did have some accuracy. Innocence was no more than an affectation with her, a season's style, unless she were a blank unmarked by experience.

I replied to her note with one of my own:

A comedy of erros [sic]? If this is The Comedy of Errors, Claire, why aren't we laughing? Or if it's eros you mean, then why not act like an adult about it? Sulk if you want to. I'm not sending flowers this time, and I won't come begging. If you want to get in touch, you've got my number.

Since she hadn't signed her note, I didn't sign mine.

Of course, the innocent victim, she exercised her right to enjoy an injured silence. I'd check my machine and find the tape blank, or Warren already going full-speed ahead at the beep.

". . . and I wanna know what you think of it. A history of, or in, epitaphs. Grave Humor, I'll call it, or Pith and Vinegar. I'd better write something now that I'm sans chair, sans, etc., etc. Here's one from Bath Abbey:

> Here lies Anne Mann; she lived an
> Old maid and died an old Mann.

"And another from Ohio, your old stomping ground:

> Under this sod
> And under these trees
> Lieth the bod-
> Y of Solomon Pease.
> He's not in this hole,
> But only his pod;
> He shelled out his soul
> And went up to God.

"Touching, huh?" Warren said. "What do you think, I should change my name to Pease? And where the fuck are you when I need you, huh?"

He sounded like he could use some help. I knew I could.

When I showed my face at his spyhole, I heard bolts sliding back and locks clicking open. "She's split," Warren said, swinging wide the door.

"Wan wai?"

"One Way," he nodded. "Weeks ago."

"She'll come back," I told him.

There were no lights on in his place. "She's already filed for divorce."

"Jeez, Warren, I'm sorry to hear it."

He had a big stogie burning in his mouth and waggled it wildly. "You think you're the only one?" He went through the routine of bolting and locking the door.

I shook my head. "Wan Wai."

"Of the laughing eyes," Warren said. "Of the thousand and one nights, less about two hundred."

I followed him through the dark hangarlike apartment that had once been a nuts and bolts factory. We made our way between a rope and board swing and an honest-to-God circus trapeze dangling from a high I-beam, and sat in director chairs facing a large, open window. He picked up a bottle from the floor, a half-empty fifth of Wild Turkey, and poured from it into a tumbler. "She wants to marry him. Can you believe that? I mean, he's older than I am, for chrissakes."

I lit a Lucky. "Who is this old guy?"

"Her gynecologist." Warren pulled a face, and laughed. "Really. I wonder what he sees in her." He handed me a tumbler of bourbon. "Ice?"

I shook my head. "Why?"

"It chills your drink," he said. I lifted my brows in a gesture of saintly patience. "I don't like it either, Bucko. Why dilute your poison?" I waited. He always made wisecracks about his troubles. The worse things were for him, the snappier his patter. A lot of my own style, I realized, I'd picked up from Warren. "One Way," he said. "She'll be his fifth wife. What a guy, huh? Caesar in the sack: I saw, I conked her, I came. Well, I'll give the old doc this much, he's a fucking optimist. Me, I'm a three-time loser. I know when to quit."

"Warren." I clapped a hand on this thick, hairy forearm and shook it. We went back a ways, Warren and I. He'd been my chairman when chairmen were chairmen. For a time he'd been chairperson before being swept from office by the department's nonsexist faction, meaning the women, in a coup led by an associate professor who'd once been his lover. Returned to the ranks, he lectured to undergrads on his specialties, The Black Death and The Reformation Era. "I've got some Valium, you need any."

"Tried and true," he said, displaying his drink. "The doc told her she had a tipped uterus. Five fucking wives. It must be a magic line. They must fall at his feet hoping he'll straighten them out."

"So what are you going to do?"

"Well, I'm not going to kill him. All's fair, etc., etc. Or me. I'm too old for that shit."

"Good." I lit another Lucky, thinking of Wan Wai, a tiny dark Malaysian with perfect legs. She'd been Warren's thesis advisee. I remembered envying him his luck when he snared her. He had asked her to move in with him, he'd said, when she refused to come see him in his office any longer. His desk was giving her a bad back. Then somehow marriage had happened to them. I watched him refill his tumbler. There were bags under his eyes, his hair was gray, he was no spring chicken. Wan Wai. He'd thought of her as an investment for his sunset years. Lines from a poem came to mind, something by Ginsberg or Corso. Should I get married? Should I be good? Then something about ending up an old man alone with pee stains on your underwear. I couldn't stop sneaking looks at Warren. He looked like an Eighth Avenue wino. "You forget to shave, or you growing a beard?"

"No, I forgot to shave, so I'm growing a beard. That's the way it happens, Bucko. It's just there, waiting to come out. Maybe this winter it'll keep me warm."

We smoked and drank. "What a gal," Warren said. "She liked to tie me down." He chuckled, fondly. "But I'd always keep one wrist loose, when she was tying the knot. When things got going, I'd pull free and turn the tables on her. She fell for it every time." He coughed, or maybe sobbed, then let out a sigh. "I am sufficiently worldly-wise to know that virtue is not rewarded, but I'm damned surprised to learn that neither is vice."

He shucked off his sandals and put his bare feet on the windowsill. Unwrapping a fresh cigar, his hands appeared uncertain. Twice he said "Fuckit!" before he got it freed and lit. I kicked off my sneakers and put my feet up too. We sat looking at the yellow glow of a street lamp. A gray haze of smoke floated in the still, hot air. "Maybe you ought to see somebody," I said. "You know."

"A shrink?" Warren laughed. "Quinn went to one, remember Quinn. His wife, his little Margie, it was her idea. Poor Quinn went from prolonged adolescence to mid-life crisis in a month. Margie, I hear, visits him at the nut farm." He picked up the bottle, poured bourbon into his tumbler, then over the hand I had covering mine. "Oops." He clunked the bottle down between our chairs. "Tipped uterus, my ass."

I cleared my throat and said, "I've broken off with Claire." I waited but Warren made no response. I resented it. I needed advice. I wanted to explain how important she was to me still, how I was willing if she was to forgive and forget. But I kept my mouth shut. Warren was staring marble-eyed at the window. Gut-shot, he hurt too much to pay attention to my flesh wound. The droop in his shoulders made me uneasy. I put gravel in my voice. "You and me, Warren, we've made a separate peace."

"Depends on how you spell it." He snorted, his way of laughing. Once it had struck me as knowing, now it sounded whipped. I lightly punched his shoulder. What could I say? Warren, old buddy, I know just how you feel; let me tell you about Claire. I lifted my tumbler as he did his, so bobbed it once, an impromptu toast. It was a bitch, my gesture suggested, the whole shooting match, but we'd stick it out, right?

On the sill his bare foot touched mine and I instinctively pulled away, although I didn't know why. If there'd ever been an unregenerate heterosexual, Warren was it. And my friend to boot. More than that, really. Not quite a father figure, not quite the older brother I'd wished for. Old army buddy maybe. Fellow vet of the battle of the sexes. We'd knock back shots and shoot the shit. Ours is not to question why. War is hell. God help me, I love it. I only regret that I have but one life. Nuts. Yankee Doodle, keep it up.

" 'They flee from me that one time did me seek,' " Warren said. "Wyatt."

"Earp." It was out before I knew it. I puffed my cheeks as if from gas.

"You know," he said, "sometimes." He drank. His life might be his joke, but not mine.

"Wyatt," I acknowledged by way of apology.

" 'Her loose gown from her shoulders did fall, and she caught me in her arms long and small.' " Eyes closed, he rested his chin on the upheld tumbler. " 'And therewith all sweetly did me kiss, and softly said, Dear heart, how like you this?' Etc., etc. So what'll it be? More of the same?"

"Me? No, I'm fine."

"You are?" he said. "Me too, I guess. Of course I'll have to find somebody else for tennis. What a service she had, huh?"

"She really did," I said. They had seemed so happy together. I'd watched them at parties touching each other in little private ways that made others envious. She'd hung on his every word. On the courts they'd gone at each other with joyful ferocity, Warren shouting Love! Fault! Douche! with such public pride.

"Up against a woman," he said, "you're always ad out. Maybe I'm better off going it alone."

I nodded. "At least you've got your freedom."

He looked at me in mock surprise, stabbing an index finger my way as if to pinpoint my genius, a gesture I'd seen him use on fatuous students. "Now that I'm single my pockets do jingle." He turned away, humming the tune.

"I only meant, it's better if you can look on it that way."

"Positive thinking, huh? Well, why not? Look at these people getting worked up about the new celibacy."

"Take it easy," I told him, gently. I wanted him to be okay, for his sake and mine. Warren had always been better at handling these things than I had, and I didn't want him falling apart on me now. I was scared too—and the strong sense of his fear brought it home harder—of ending up without a woman. Of being weak, of getting old, of crying in my suds over lost loves. Of acting, I realized with a pang of traitorous guilt, the way Warren was now. He couldn't handle his liquor like he used to. More and more often he called on me to help him through some present crisis—a lover who felt bound to tell all to her husband, a student who feared she was pregnant, a wife's desertion. Lately I'd taken to observing him covertly as though this man's life which I'd once thought exemplary might in fact be cautionary.

"I mean, look at that poor fucker." My eyes followed his pointing finger. Across the street from us was a brick apartment house. It was a hive of graduate students; I'd known a girl there once. Framed in one of the lit windows a thin boy, a young man I suppose, sat at a desk reading and taking notes. His head was bent to the task. A green-shaded desk lamp put a plate of light on his open book. Warren consulted the glowing face of his wristwatch. "Nearly showtime, Bucko." I tried to estimate just how drunk he was. I still wanted to bring up Claire, but doubted this was the time. I wished I had called him earlier; I'd been meaning to, but one thing or the other, hadn't gotten around to it. It was hard for men to keep in touch when women took up all their time.

"Better than TV," he said.

I said, "What isn't?"

Warren spat. "No, there, you think I been wanting you to come over here so I could cry on your shoulder? I wanted you to see this. Lookit." I looked and saw then that a woman had entered the student's room. She wore a bluish nightgown wispy enough to make the old dog of my libido look up and salivate. She was young and her reddish hair was short and wavy. "She must work evenings. It's always about now she shows up."

The woman's presence in the room made the studious boy seem sad, or tired, like one of Edward Hopper's aged men in undershirts. She came up behind the boy, young man, and rubbed his neck. It surprised me that he didn't turn around. Who did he think he was fooling? She kept rubbing his neck. The light seemed to ricochet from the desk to reflect her blue figure. I said, "I'll be damned."

"Every fucking night," Warren said, his speech slurred. The girl fitted herself between the reader and the text. With what seemed resignation, he held her on his lap. She kissed him twice before, on the third go, he put any effort into returning it. Did he really think he was fooling her? She reached out a hand and turned off the magic lantern.

I felt embarrassed, even shamed, by what I had seen, which struck me as odd given all I've seen and done. I asked Warren for the time, but he didn't appear to hear me. He refilled his tumbler and took a long, hard drink of it. Lifting the bottle, he held it in the street lamp's light. He had killed it. His breathing had taken on that labored wet sound that comes from pneumonia or intensive boozing. The room seemed more than dark; it had a brooding gloom. "Of course," Warren said suddenly, "no one can save you."

I looked away, and waited, I didn't know what for. Warren stared dead ahead. I guessed that he was waiting, or hoping, for the window across the way to light up again. Maybe that too was part of the nightly show. Suddenly I was seized with a need near panic to get out into the open air. I pulled on my sneakers and patted my friend's shoulder. "I'll be in touch."

The first thing I did at home was to turn on all the lights, the second was to call Claire. Just before she hung up, I cried, "Please, marry me!"

The days dragged by. I ran in the park, but only in a circle. Claire didn't want to see me, I didn't want to see Warren. Hell, I didn't want to see *me* either, but I was stuck with my company. And with thinking of Claire. Bad enough that my heart was riddled with guilt and regret, but my gonads kept prompting the projectionist in my brain to rerun the color footage of the night she'd spent with me. With each showing the action seemed better. Why had I ever thought she was a disappointment? The magic I'd thought her presence lacked, her absence now proved. And who in the world was I to require innocence?

I sat in my apartment at night waiting for her to call or appear. The way I saw it, I had no choice but to wait her out; that's what I said I would do and if I didn't she'd always think I was bluffing. This was trench warfare and it wore a man down. My hair started falling out. Every morning after my shower I scraped a skein of it from the drain. The crinkles at the corners of my eyes no longer came and went with laughter, but stayed put, no laughing matter. Decline was inevitable. I gave up jogging. I smoked day and night. I played her record albums and got falling-down drunk. I took to walking the streets. I frequented peep shows. I hung out downtown in Washington Square, that unending United Nations picnic, hoping for and dreading a chance to spot my ex-wife and her beau.

In the middle of another barren week, I drowned my sorrows at a Blarney Stone before stumbling home. In the lobby, I found a neighbor, Honey, buzzing my apartment. "Oh," she said, "I thought you just weren't answering." A singer and dancer, she lived with a piano player in the apartment below mine. I'd heard them making music at all hours. I dropped my keys, picked them up, and she took my arm to steady me. Her green net top gave me a peek at piquant nipples. A pink trout fly dangled from one earlobe.

"You're locked out?"

"No," she said, "Peter and I had a falling out, sort of."

"Honey." I shook my head in commiseration.

"So I wondered if, you know, you could like, put me up. Just for tonight."

Later, I lay awake in my bed beside her bare young body, at my indecent leisure taking in those wonderfully long slim legs and the russet triangle of fuzz which only a short time previous had provided me with a brief peace. I didn't feel peaceful now. I was troubled that I felt no emotional connection to this woman sleeping beside me. Like her name, Honey afforded instant intimacy, but one that remained curiously public in nature. Our coupling had possessed all the romance of a Black and Decker drilling a mannequin. If the act itself is essentially meaningless, I thought, no more than the transfer of a teaspoon of semen that is, why do I persist in ceaselessly repeating it with the hope that it might lead to something transcendent? Unless it's because it's the only trick I know. In which case I was going through the first grade twelve times in a row expecting to receive my high school diploma.

Yet I knew that this night could be narrated—would be in fact—in such a way as to delight and impress others, Warren especially. The lady found abandoned on the hero's doorstep. The wild night. In fact it seemed to me that the recounting of the adventure would have more felt reality than the drunken incidents making it up. Maybe that gay fop Oscar Wilde was being more true than witty when he said, Anybody can make history; only a great man can write it. Yet Napoleon, and who'd know better, claimed history was only a fable agreed upon. Worse yet, there was Goethe: Sins write histories; goodness is silent. Put a lid on it, I told myself. Your mind will fuck with you, but won't come to anything. But it was too late. I'd opened the way for doubts and fears, that mental rabble of sleepless nights. Anxiety mounted in me until it prompted me to again mount my overnight guest. History might be a nightmare from which we were trying to awake, but undoubtedly my life was a history from which I hoped dreams would release me. So I used the uncomplaining Honey as a nightcap to induce sleep, perchance to dream. If there's a bottom to hit in all this, I thought, achieving a second, joyless release, this must be it.

I was wrong about that. Sometime during the night I started awake to see Claire standing at the foot of my bed, my key in her hand. I blinked and she was gone. A dream? I was too exhausted to move or think. I fell back on the bed and hoped I'd been sleeping through all of it.

In the morning I found my extra key on the hall floor. By the time I'd roused the sluggish Honey and got her packed off, took a shower and shaved and had a Valium and orange juice, it was noon. When I called Claire's office they told me she was no longer with them. "Since when?" I cried, but I'd already been disconnected. I got dressed and, steady as a house of cards, stood at the curb waiting for a bus, to take it or throw myself under it, whichever the moment called for.

There was a stack of cardboard boxes in front of her apartment door. The door itself was ajar. How naive can one person be, how stupid? Unless she was begging to get raped. I stepped inside and saw Claire on her hands and knees, her back to me, scrubbing the hall floor. She wore jean cut-offs and a yellow halter top. "Who is it?" she called. A perfect ass, my brain noted before the censor could kick in; not now, for chrissakes, this is serious.

"Claire," I said. She jumped to her feet. Her knees were reddened, and so were her eyes. A blue bandana tied back her hair. She looked so homey, so vulnerable, I wanted to weep.

"You son of a bitch!" She ran past me to lock herself in the bathroom.

"Please," I said at the door. "I have to see you. I want to talk to you, about us, I want to explain."

"Oh go away."

I looked down the hall. There were more boxes in the living room, some of them filled with her things. Where did she think she was going? I raised a fist to pound on the bathroom door just as it opened. Her hands flew up and she flinched. Then she reached out to hold my face in her hands. I waited for her to kiss me, but she just held me and looked at me. Her touch lifted my spirits a bit. We were still possible. I would help her unpack. The bleach on her hands stung my nose, and my eyes watered. "Please, listen to me."

"No, you listen. I know it's not all your fault. I came over last night to say I was sorry, I should have told you everything earlier."

"But, it doesn't matter now. I don't care."

"I'm sorry now that I came," she said. "I wanted to tell you that you taught me something. This isn't the place for me. I knew it but didn't want to admit it. I'm leaving."

"Where?"

"No," she said. "No. I can't tell you now. But I won't forget the good things we had. Now go, goodbye, it's over."

"Claire, please!" My face still in her hands, she backed me to the door, through it and into the hall. "If you leave me, what will I do?"

"Go home."

"I can't."

"Yes," she said, "you can. Take the subway. Go downstairs and go to the corner. You'll see a hole in the ground. Go into it." She closed the door and bolted it.

What Hemingway said about Paris is true of New York. There is never any ending to it, though that was the end of a part of it for me. New York was never to be the same again although it was always New York and I changed as it changed.

My classes resumed. In the face of human history, I told my students, the only proper response is to laugh. They laughed.

Honey and her pianist made music again.

I made a scene at a faculty party, drunkenly crooning "Andy Scruder," but this being Manhattan the other guests only chuckled, a sound like geese gagging.

A neighbor gave me a cat which I named Cat for Cat Stevens. It sat on my lap and plucked my thighs with its claws. I hardly noticed, numbed as I was by aquavit taken from the bottle sip by sip, deliberate, spiteful, and bittersweet, as over and over again a voice golden with hope sang that morning has broken. What on earth had I hoped for? That it might be like the first morning, despite my knowing all history is a lesson in ruin?

After three more rejections of my military defeats book I filed it away.

Late that fall I hit forty. It brought no wisdom. It felt like the morning after a thirty-nine-year bender.

Later that fall Warren tried to hang himself using the trapeze in some way but he slipped out of the noose, or the knot slipped, something slipped, and he had a bad fall. At the hospital I looked at the floor and Warren—in traction and a body cast—looked at the ceiling. "Hey, numb-nuts," he said, "here's one for you. Joseph Eve, His Epitaph:

> Here rests one whom fortune never favored,
> Who grew no wiser from the past;
> But e'er with perseverance labored
> And still contended to the last.

I think I'll have them put that on my stone."

I told him, "You're not going to die."

"No, nor walk. Doc says it's a wheelchair for me. On the plus side, he says, I'll be numb below the waist. I'm whores de combat, Bucko. Women, God love them, it took them fifty-two years but they finally won. Maybe now I'll have some peace."

I sat with him for a while, talking about the Giants and his disability benefits. I couldn't bring myself to ask if he planned to try again. I gave him a pack of fat cigars, which he hid under his pillow.

"Keep your powder dry," I said. He gave me a thumbs-up.

Claire wrote to me one time. Her letter was typed on yellow paper and riddled with errors. There was no return address.

Please don't try to find me, it won't do either of us any good. I'm not going to try to explain what happened to us. ~~I don't have all your education and so can't put in all your learned illusions.~~ I just want to try to be happy. ~~I know you can't understand.~~ I'm working outside the city now, editing a news letter for an order of nuns, seriously, no joke. They do chairty work and I help with fund raising and recruting. ~~I think I can learn to be good at this.~~ I've got a third floor apartment in a wonderful old Victorian house. Theres beautiful countryside all around, the air is so clean here, its so quiet, and there are alot of white birches. I take long walks in the woods. I think its helping me develope my spirtuality. I'm learning to like independance. I can barely wait for snow so I can ski! Take care.

Nearing the close of this historical account, I recognize that the heart of it seems to be missing, that heart being Claire or perhaps love. There are reasons for this absence, I think. Claire remained a mystery to me despite my avid tinkering with her various parts. Maybe I'd caught one glimpse of her meaning, that more important than innocence was her capacity for renewal, her ability to sustain belief in the possibility of a fresh start. If I knew how to reach her, I'd tell her this now.

As for love, considering my behavior, I guess it didn't happen. Maybe it didn't have a chance to happen. I remember studying Kant's categories once, thinking that somehow they might be applicable to historical order. All that remains of that now is an image I have of a row of letter boxes in a rural post office. Addressed mail goes into the labeled box accordingly. If a letter should arrive bearing a name for which there is no corresponding box, it's sent back or ends up in the dead letter bin. Whichever, it doesn't connect. So in fact it never properly arrives. It must be something like that with human beings—with ideas and emotions, I mean. No box, no mail. Maybe I don't have a box labeled *love*. There's *lust*, *romance*, and *sentiment*: I take whatever comes into those as being all the mail there is. So much for my philosophy studies. From Kant to cunt, as Warren might say.

My point is that this account is less about the object of what I called my love than it is about my failure to do whatever I ought to have done to make love possible. There is no history, Emerson wrote, only biography. Today of course it's all autobiography. *Self, Us, People*, they know where our true interests lie. Each of us hungers for Mystory.

I still dream of Claire, sleeping or waking. I sit on the sofa where I held her and had her, and I imagine how it might have been with us if the right balance had been struck between need and freedom, possession and loss; if I'd been able to call forth from myself something worthy of her naive belief in good in a person. I conjure up all sorts of happy endings, but they all depend on me being someone other than I am. Maybe if Claire had gotten pregnant and died in childbirth, like Catherine Barkley in *A Farewell To Arms*, that might have made for a satisfactory, if not quite happy, ending. Then I could have walked out of the hospital into the empty night street, a perseverant figure grown larger than life in my fight with the fates.

Instead I fucked it up, and she split.

Over and over again I review our time together, trying to record its various incidents, as if studied enough it will reveal something truly significant. Yet the more I look at it, the less meaning it seems to possess. The memory steadily diminishes until it is only a souvenir from the front, and my recounting of it becomes just another war story: We got in there, man, and it was hot; it was un-fucking-believable.

As Papa wrote shortly before his shotgun exit: "All truly wicked things start from an innocence. You lie and hate it and it destroys you and every day is more dangerous, but you live day to day as in a war."

Then it was winter in the city.

Gaming

There was no front way to Lucy Wenner's. The long outside flight of gray wooden stairs led to the kitchen door. Once the back door, it was now the only one, for the apartment was half its former self. The living room and bedroom had been blocked off long before Lucy moved in to form an office above the downstairs barber shop. A lawyer just out of school held the office now. He was so young, Price thought, he still talked about justice instead of law.

Russ Price, wearing clean green twill workpants and a pressed white shirt, tieless and open-collared, waited before the kitchen door. Behind him, the stairs creaked under the monstrous weight of Marty Conkling.

Violet shadows of early evening relieved the drabness of the gray porch and wall. A high small kitchen window was pale yellow with light, the four square panes like pats of margarine.

Price couldn't count the times he'd stood at this door waiting for Lucy to open it. She had lived in the apartment seven years now, ever since Bill, her husband, died in the fire of his jack-knifed tanker. Bill and Price had been good friends.

Marty succeeded in mounting the stairs. He stood sucking wind, his face beaded in sweat like a basted turkey.

"What if she gets mad? She could call the cops."

Price waved him into silence and rapped his knuckles against the door. It opened to linoleum and a hanging bare bulb. A boy of six hung on the knob.

"Hello, Lucky," Price said.

"Who is it, Russell?" a woman's voice asked.

The boy turned. "Mister Price."

"Whiteshirt?" Lucy came into the light. She had tinted her hair reddish in the months since Price had last caught sight of her downtown. To cover gray? he wondered. His own hair showed salt and pepper at the temples now. His face had creased with the strain of forty-eight years of managing day-to-day life.

By now she had to be at least forty.

But she was still a woman a man noticed, even in the cotton house dress she wore. Her body's fullness seemed to offer a man ease. Though Price knew better.

"What brings you here?"

"See how you are."

"Sure."

"Lucky," Price said to the boy, "you're shooting up like a weed."

"Who's your friend?" Lucy asked.

"Marty. He works with me."

Marty leaned to one side to look past Price's shoulder. "Hi," he said.

"Hi."

"Pleased to meet you."

"You want to come in?" Lucy said to Price.

"If you're not busy."

"I'm home from work, why should I be busy?"

"You want me to go?"

"I didn't say that." Lucy took a step back and motioned them in. Marty sidled to the refrigerator and leaned his back against it, studying the floor. Price stood in the center of the room.

Two girls in their early teens sat at the kitchen table with the boy. They had been playing Monopoly. They frowned at the interruption, and Price saw that they had Bill's eyebrows.

"Who's winning?" he asked.

"Mom," one of the girls said.

"Figures. You got a head for business, Lucy."

"Look who's talking." She had tugged straight the faded green dress and tightened its belt. She brushed back her hair with one hand.

"She's got Boardwalk and Park Place," the other girl said. "Houses on them, too."

"Can we play?" the boy whined. "It's my turn!"

"In a bit, Russell," Lucy said. Then to Price, "You want to watch us play or what?"

"I'd like to talk to you."

"Go ahead."

Price moved past her, going into the adjoining room. "Wait just a minute," she was saying.

The room was a combined living and bed room. It had two windows and Price stepped to one to look down at an alley. He heard Lucy telling the children to go ahead and play. She came into the room and shut the door.

"What's the big idea?"

He didn't look at her. He thought he could feel the heat of her body. "How you been doing?"

"What's it to you?"

"You make enough at the plant to go along?"

"I do just fine."

"Got plenty of friends there probably."

"What if I do?"

He turned and looked down at her. "Don't get me wrong. What you do is your business."

"I know that."

"I'm not asking for myself."

"Asking what?"

"If you're still in business."

"You sonuvabitch!"

"Take it easy," Price said. "It's nothing to me one way or the other."

"Sure."

"It isn't. I just wanted to know."

"Who for?"

Price jerked his head at the door. Lucy's eyebrows jumped. "You got to be kidding."

"He'll end up in a nuthouse unless some woman treats him right."

"You're crazy, Whiteshirt."

"Look, we're grown up, right?"

"I can only speak for myself."

"Let's not fight about it. I hear him every day, whining. No woman will look at him twice. He's a sick kid. He needs help."

"Take him to a doctor."

"Have a heart."

"You can say that to me? To *me?*"

"Keep your voice down, will you?"

"Here we go again. 'Keep your voice down, Lucy. Act like nothing's wrong, Lucy. Take it easy, Lucy.'"

Price stepped away from the window. "I thought I'd be doing you a favor."

"Sure."

"You need the money, don't you?"

Lucy's open hand smacked against his cheek, knocking loose two strands of his black forelock. Price didn't move.

"Big-hearted, aren't you? You low bastard!"

"Canning season's almost over, isn't it? You got another job lined up?"

"I get along without any help from you. Believe me, I don't need it. I don't need you one bit. Not for anything."

Price sighed. He smoothed his hair back in place and briefly touched his cheek. "I just thought maybe the charity wasn't enough."

"Don't try to rub my nose in it, Whiteshirt, because it won't work. Not anymore."

"What do you mean?"

"It's A.D.C. I'm a citizen, I got rights. I get nothing but what I'm entitled to. Less, if you ask me. If Bill's pension was better . . ."

"Maybe we'd never have gotten together."

Lucy stepped forward, her shoulders sagging. "You make me be so hard with you. You never give me a chance to be anything else. Your whore! All you had to do, Whiteshirt, was to say yes."

"You're forgetting how it was. I told you the best thing to do. All you had to do was do it."

"I may not be much, Whiteshirt, but I'm no baby-killer."

"And I'm no family man. Like I told you." Price turned to walk slowly about the room. Beyond the couch and easy chair facing the TV, there were bunk beds and a large brown pasteboard wardrobe. A curtained alcove held, he knew, Lucy's bed. "I guess I'll go."

"I'm old enough to be his mother," Lucy said.

"And I could be his father. So what?"

"I'm getting too old."

"Quit feeling sorry for yourself."

"If I don't, who will? You?"

"Look, you're not hurting me by saying no. Go look at him. The poor slob's ready to cut his throat or hang himself."

"Let him." Her upper lip curled. "Listen, I'm onto you. You don't lord it over me anymore, hear?"

"What do you think I'm trying to pull? I'm trying to help out is all."

"You? You never cared about anybody. . . . Where you going?"

"I didn't come to hear a sermon."

"Wait a minute."

"What for?"

"Maybe I'll do it."

"So make up your mind."

"Not for the money though. Or for him. For you, Russ."

"What the hell are you talking about? It's him wants it, not me."

"For you—as a favor. Ask me nice. Say please."

"For Chrissakes."

"I'm not kidding, Whiteshirt. Ask me, say please, or get the hell out."

"I just don't understand you."

"You never did. Well?"

"All right. Sure. *Please.* You satisfied?"

"Tell him to come in."

Price opened the door and called to Marty. The fat boy hurried across the kitchen. "Look," he whispered, "if she don't . . ."

"It's all right. Come on."

"I could hear you, she was arguing. I don't wanna cause any trouble."

"It's all set." Price looked at the children. "Who's winning?"

"Nobody yet," one of the girls said.

"Where's Mom?" the boy asked.

"She'll be right out. Got to talk about something." He hissed to Marty, "You want it or not? Come on. She'll treat you right."

"I don't know. You were arguing."

Price took Marty's arm and pulled him into the room. "I wanna go," Marty whispered.

Lucy had gone to the alcove, now she returned. She was still wearing her dress, but Price noticed her shoes were gone. He guessed that she'd taken off her panties, too.

"Go on." He pushed Marty toward her.

The fat boy stood for a moment, stranded, then Lucy came to him and took his hands in hers. "Marty," she said. "I'll bet you're strong as an ox."

Price was intrigued by her crisp movements, and the certainty in her voice. She seemed alert, self-possessed, a professional.

This was the woman he needed to remember. This was how she was when he first met her, before her softening into slumped shoulders, her eyes puffed from crying, her belly beginning to swell.

"Watch the door for us, will you?" Lucy asked.

Price moved to go into the kitchen.

"No, in here. The girls will think something's funny if you leave us in here alone."

"He's not gonna stay?" Marty's voice rose to a squeal.

"He has to," Lucy said. "My girls."

"I don't want him staying."

"He won't look. Will you, Whiteshirt?"

"No," Price said.

"See? Now come on, come over here." Lucy led Marty to the alcove. He waited for her to arrange the bed, but instead she asked him to lie down on the floor. He tried to back away. Price looked at the ceiling.

"No offense, honey," Lucy was saying, "but the bed, well, it's small, don't you see? If we break it, where would I sleep? You don't want me to have to sleep on the floor, do you?" She kept up a soothing banter as she managed, like a mahout training an elephant calf, to get the boy down on the floor. "You're too big a man to be on top. You see what I mean, don't you. You don't want to hurt me now, do you? And I won't hurt you either. Here, it's all right. Let me get your belt."

Marty lay on his back with his head toward Price. Lucy knelt beside him in the interior dusk, her hands working, then slid her dress up her thighs and settled onto the boy like a hen onto an egg. She began rocking slowly. "There," she said, her eyes on Price. "How's that? Nice, huh?"

The fat boy grunted. His arms were outspread, and his hands flat on the floor. He looked like a beached swimmer, Lucy a lifeguard working to revive him.

Price imagined her thighs beneath the airy fan of her skirt pressed sweating about the fat boy's hips. He could hear the smack of her wet flesh, like a suction cup drawing out poison. He couldn't keep his eyes off her. Skilled in her craft, she worked with an efficiency beyond shame.

Price felt himself warm and grow. He tugged at the stiff fly of his trousers and was caught off-guard by Lucy's laugh.

The bitch, he thought.

He straightened and leaned back against the door, folding his arms across his chest.

Behind him he heard a girl's voice claim eight hundred dollars rent—"it has four houses"—and the boy begging her to accept the Utilities in trade so he could stay in the game.

Price met Lucy's look. He smiled to show his lack of discomfort.

"That's fine," Lucy said. "You're doing just fine, honey."

She leaned forward to pull Marty's hands from the floor. She planted them against her covered breasts where they stuck like barnacles. Her hands on Marty's shoulders, she began pumping up and down. The fat boy whimpered. Lucy bared her teeth in a grin.

Price felt a sudden surprising rush of anger at the boy enjoying a woman he had no right to even look at.

He checked his anger. What did right have to do with it? A man got what he paid for.

He knew her game, and swore she wouldn't make him jealous. Anyone misses what's gone, he thought, but only a fool tries to go back.

In you want out; out you want in.

Price watched the two figures on the floor. He forced down reawakened feelings as if suffocating them with a pillow; he etched in his mind the wrinkles about her eyes, and the sag of flesh beneath her chin.

Some prize, he thought. Wearing out with use. No wonder she wants somebody to take care of her.

How would her girls take it when they learned the truth? And the boy, poor little bastard, a whore for a mother? What could any father say to change that?

They sat at a table to the rear of the Tin Cup, Price with his back to the wall. He ordered a Strohs for each of them and a shot of

Old Grandad for himself. He held up the shot glass between thumb and forefinger, dipping his head to look through the clear amber at the soft round face opposite him. "Here's to you, a man of the world." He downed the shot like medicine.

Marty managed a clownish smile.

Price slowly poured beer from the bottle into his glass. A half-inch head rose above the rim and held there, a contained quavering. "Hear about the whores got mad at the bartender for putting salt in their Schlitz?"

"Uh-uh." Marty ran two fingers around and around the lip of his glass.

"It's a joke, dummy."

"Oh."

"Drink your beer. You earned it."

"You pay her?"

"I left it on the dresser."

"She said not to."

"She was kidding."

"How do you know?"

"I know."

"Why would she say it if she didn't mean it?"

"Women. Who knows?"

Marty's bulk swayed to one side as if he had to pass gas. He dug in a back pocket. "I'll pay you back."

"Forget it."

"I wanna." He opened a worn black billfold.

"You can buy the drinks."

"It was more."

"Forget it. Maybe now you can keep your mind on your work, not have me picking up for you."

"What d'you mean? I work."

"Who you kiddin? You been mooning around like a sick cow. I load more packages in an hour than you do in a day. You want to pay me back, keep up your end."

"I try to."

"Then do it. You got your piece now. Relax."

Marty's eyes took on a hurt look. He drank from his glass, then began toying with it again. "I wish I was married."

"To her?"

Marty shrugged. "She's nice."

"On what you make? What'd you have her do, take in boarders? Like the landlady caught spreading roomers?"

"Hey, c'mon!"

"Some husband you'd make! Save your money for Friday nights, you're better off."

"I don't know."

"I know you don't know, dummy, that's why I'm telling you."

Price wasn't surprised that the fat boy was hooked. Lucy was a woman to make a man feel alive. "You couldn't find a better woman than Lucy," Bill used to tell Price. "In every way." "I believe it," Price would say, envying his friend's good luck.

Closing his eyes, he pictured Bill burning in the wreck's fireball, turning to ash. The way had seemed clear, then. If only a man had shoulders broad enough to carry the load.

Price ordered another round. Each night he had two beers, two shots, never any more, even when someone else was buying. He'd seen too many of the old boys bellying up, day and night, slaves to booze.

A foundry worker sat at the bar. The man's face and hands were a powdery black. Price watched him take a long drink of his beer, then wipe his lips to leave an ash-gray blur about his mouth.

All the Tin Cup regulars were burnt-out, Price thought. Like old houses whose furnaces got too hot.

Stoke it, stoke it, that heat feels oh so good!

The foundry man stared at his big-knuckled blackened hands as if they were clinkers raked from the ashes.

Price glanced at Marty. What could he know? A hog, he wanted it all. He'd be another one bellyaching about bills, the wife's female troubles, the girl with measles, how there was nothing could straighten out that boy, stealing hubcaps now, and who knew what next.

None of them knew anything. Their heads were to hold their hats.

In the morning Price would leave his room at six-fifteen, have one egg over, dry toast, black coffee and a small grapefruit juice. At seven he punched in. On the dock, lucky to be in parcels rather than freight, he would load, stopping twice for coffee and once for lunch, until three-thirty. His evenings he had to himself.

"Hey, Whiteshirt!"

A barmaid was pointing at him. Price started up, then sat, seeing the small figure threading the tables to him.

The boy stopped beside Price's chair. He looked down at his ratty black sneakers.

"Psst," Marty whispered. "Isn't this her kid?"

" 'Course it's her kid. Whose kid you think it is?"

The boy looked too thin to Price. Was she so bitter she begrudged him food? "Too late for you to be out, Lucky," he said. "You ought to be home in bed."

The boy unclenched a fist and dropped two crumpled ten dollar bills onto the table.

"What do you think you're doing?" When the boy flinched, Price softened his voice. "Your mom tell you to do this?"

The boy nodded.

"What'd I tell you," Marty said. "Didn't I tell you she didn't want it?"

"Shuttup."

"But I was right, wasn't I?"

"Shuttup before I toss your fat ass outta here." Price lay a hand on the boy's bony shoulder. "I don't want this. This belongs to your mom."

"She said."

Why send the boy? The girls were older; one of them should have come.

"She said you can't come see us anymore."

Did she hate him that much? How could she say she loved him for what he was and yet hate him for what he was?

"I knew she was mad," Marty started, but Price waved him into silence. He picked up the two bills and flattened them against the table with the palm of a hand, slowly smoothing them back and forth. The boy moved to go. "Hold it," Price said. He lay one bill atop the other, folded the two in halves, quarters, eighths. He stuck the small green wad into the boy's jean pocket and pushed his hand away.

"Lucky, this is going to be our secret. Just between us. I was a good friend of your daddy. He asked me to help look after you. So that money's yours. You keep it. Hide it someplace. You don't have to tell your mom, she won't know. It's yours. You need it sometime, you'll have it. You understand what I'm telling you?"

The boy nodded.

"And something else. You got to get your sleep and eat right, you want to grow up strong. You listening to me?"

"She said she liked it," the boy said. "I'm supposed to tell you."

"What?"

"She said you'd know." The boy turned to Marty. "And to tell you thanks."

Marty grinned widely.

"Well, goddamn!" Price said. He patted the boy's shoulder. "You get on home and get to bed. Go on now."

When the boy had gone, Price sipped his beer in silence. Twice Marty cleared his throat as if to speak. Finally he asked, "How come you gave him the money? Lucy said . . ."

"Lucy? Shit!"

"Well she said she didn't want any money, didn't she? Maybe she just wanted to have some fun."

"It's my weakness," Price said. "Yours is being stupid, mine's being big-hearted." He emptied his glass and leaned back in the chair. "I am a generous man."

Father's Day

Since the women had taken the Matador to Saint Mary's for the late Mass, Dewey had to ask to use Russell's Luv. It lacked a bumper hitch so they loaded the log splitter using a ramp of planks. It was a ten horsepower Lickety Split. The little blue pickup sagged on its springs. Dewey had taken the precaution of laying quarter-inch plywood in the bed. Rust had eaten the Luv clear through in spots.

"You ought to get some naval jelly." Dewey ground out his cigarette with a foot. He breathed with his mouth open. "And weld sheet metal behind the wheel wells."

Russell twitched his lips, showing teeth.

Margaret's father, when Dewey married into her family, had taken to calling him "son." Dewey could not bring himself to call Mickey's Russell that. He couldn't think of Mickey as Mrs. Wenner either. "The thing of it is," he said, "it'll eat your truck right out from under you."

Russell got in and started the engine.

Dewey stood braced against the tailgate, sucking air. His light blue eyes watered as if he'd just been struck in the nose. He took out a white handkerchief and wiped sweat from his neck and forehead. Fifty-four and he was shot to heck. He got into the tiny cab and slammed the door, wincing at the tinny sound. The pink bedspread covering the bench seat wadded up beneath him and he lifted up to yank it smooth. He put his pack of Lucky Strikes on the vinyl dash. "Anymore, it seems I can't work worth a darn."

Russell pulled out of the drive. Sunday, and he wore an army fatigue shirt with the sleeves hacked off at the shoulder, though he hadn't been in anybody's army that Dewey knew of, and a strip of white towel as a sweatband. He played the slipping clutch to get up speed. It might be the slave cylinder, Dewey knew, but more likely the pressure plate was shot.

"I guess I got enough gas."

Dewey craned his neck to eye the gauge. "You're all right."

"Just so we don't come back empty."

"I'll keep an eye on it."

Russell turned onto Sandusky Street, Olentangy's main drag. Even with the truck windows open the mill smell coming from him was potent: beet pulp and molasses. There was nothing sweet about it to Dewey. And there was no getting it out of Russell's outfits, Mickey told Margaret, though why the boy wore work clothes on a Sunday when he wasn't even working anymore, Dewey had no idea.

"You wouldn't say no to some breakfast, would you?"

Russell said no, he wouldn't say no.

It went without saying who was buying. Last week Dewey and Margaret had stopped in to see Mickey, and had dropped off the little black and white Zenith as a gift. Dewey had never cared for the orange cabinet and the picture had taken to rolling, but it was a lot better than nothing if that was what you had. Mickey acted happy about it, but Russell hardly took notice. You have to understand, Margaret said, a young man like that has his pride. Dewey understood pride was a thing you worked to earn.

The night's hard rain had knocked the blossoms off the big catalpa tree in front of Swope's Cafe. The white petals lay in a ring around the trunk, making Dewey think of a wedding cake.

Edith Swope was working the grill. Air from a ceiling fan

fluttered her henna curls. Dewey mounted a stool at the counter and Russell dropped down beside him.

"Happy Father's Day," Edith called.

Russell piped up. "No kids of mine around I know about."

"Thank you," Dewey said to Edith. He inquired about Ed, and Edith said he was coming along as well as could be expected.

Tough as oak, Ed Swope had cancer. Anymore it was painful to look at him, hollowed out like he'd been hit by carpenter ants. He used to have a beer with Dewey at the bowling alley, Thursday nights, after the league. Some motorcycle boys came in one time, mother-this, mother-that, and Dewey struck one on the forehead with an Old Milwaukee. Ed took care of the others. For a time Dewey and Ed were made out to be hell-raisers, but Dewey shrugged it off. It was a thing that happened and was over before you knew it. Ten years ago? He shook his head. Fifteen?

A well-endowed young woman with shoulders broad enough to buck hay came to take their order. She was a new face to Dewey. "What?" she said.

Russell asked the girl why she didn't sweet talk the Swopes into getting air-conditioning.

"Coffee," Dewey said. "Cream, please, and a cinnamon stick." The usual, he'd have told Lou.

The girl jotted it on her pad without so much as a glance his way. It appeared she thought Russell somebody worth noticing. Her eyes were greenish-gray with an odd cast to them. They put Dewey to mind of a goat's eyes.

Russell wanted a large milk, three eggs over, sausage, home fries, and a double order of toast. "Wheat, not white—or you get no tip, sweet stuff."

"You watch yourself," the girl said, grinning. "Else I just might bite you on the kneecap."

Russell hooted. He rapidly slapped the flat of his palms on the counter, like somebody playing the bongos.

After the girl brought their order and wandered off, Dewey asked, "What sort of a remark was that?"

Russell shrugged.

"I think that girl may be retarded." Dewey added one teaspoon of sugar to his coffee. He swiveled about on his stool. "Where's Lou?"

"Flu," Edith said.

"Tell her I said to get well." Dewey ate his cinnamon stick, dabbing at his lips with a paper napkin. He took care not to dribble coffee on himself. He wore a cotton knit shirt, burgundy, with a little blue fox on the left breast. Mickey had given it to him last year for Father's Day. The color had faded but the shirt fit well; his shoulders filled it square to the seams and he had no belly to stretch it out of shape. His blue-checked slacks, beltless with a Ban-Rol band, were a size thirty-two waist. Margaret liked to tease by calling him a dandy. Dewey didn't mind. The navy had taught him a man ought to mind his appearance.

Russell mopped up egg and sausage with his toast. Like the rest of his people, a pack of hilligans, he had no more manners than a hog. Dewey picked up his Luckies and went to the register. Goat Eyes rang up the tickets. From his change, Dewey left her a quarter.

Russell made a show of flipping coins onto the counter. He laughed like it was a joke. So did the retarded girl.

Outside, Dewey lit a cigarette. "We don't want to be all day," he said when Russell finally showed. "Margaret is putting in a turkey loaf after church."

They drove out of town along River Road. Dewey clicked on the radio. He moved the needle until he brought in the Big Band Bash. The Andrews sisters sang "Boogie Woogie Bugle Boy from Company B," which made him smile. There was a weather bulletin about small stream and urban flooding. It was the rainiest June since Dewey didn't know when. He tapped his fingers on his thigh to Benny Goodman's "Sing Sing Sing." "Could that man play the licorice stick!"

"How far is it?" Russell wanted to know.

It was ten miles out, a long yellow brick with huge picture

windows that Margaret called her dream house. It belonged to a man Dewey's age, a lawyer named Moore with a white Coupe de Ville and, so went the talk at Swope's, a liking for his liquor and for another man's wife. The mess some people made of their lives. But the man always offered Dewey a drink, which he declined, and paid in cash, which he appreciated. He did not, however, care for the crack about letting the tax man look out for himself. No one could find fault with the records Dewey kept.

He directed Russell around back where they unloaded the Lickety Split, working it in between a riding mower and a snow blower, then had him wait in the truck while he collected.

"He pay you?" was the first thing out of Russell's mouth. He puffed on a Lucky.

Dewey slammed his door. He took his cigarettes from the dash. "Sure he paid me." There was no use trying to explain to the boy that men of Dewey's generation paid their debts without question. Dewey wedged his wallet into a back pocket. He'd charged fifteen for labor, cleared ten on the new hydraulic pump, and tacked on five for delivery. He'd thought to buy Russell some gas, but had changed his mind after laying out three-fifty for breakfast. How the boy could eat so much and stay so skinny, Dewey had no idea.

Russell backed down the long, curving drive. He had switched radio stations; rock guitars screamed like tomcats fighting.

On River Road Dewey spotted a surprising number of "Lot for Sale" signs. It would be all houses before long. Then people would move further out and get that all built up. Anymore the way things were going, Olentangy would be a part of Columbus by the time Mickey's kids were grown. Dewey could recall when it was a big trip to go into Columbus. They used to take Mickey to the petting zoo. She liked to feed the lambs, and would hide behind his leg, holding up her cone of feed to keep the pushy goats from getting it all.

Russell suggested they pick up some beer.

They were approaching a cement block building painted aqua and advertising "Amih Food." Meaning Amish, Dewey

knew. The carryout was run by a Vietnamese family, not a one
of whom could spell. Dewey didn't know why they didn't sell
egg rolls. "We might do that," he said.

Russell swung across the road and braked in the lot. "How
about some Rolling Rock?"

Dewey took his cigarettes with him. He told the refugee
woman to keep the sack. He carried the six pack of cans under
one arm like a football, side-stepping rain puddles. He'd been
one heck of a blocking back in his time.

"No Rolling Rock?"

"Old Dutch."

Russell pulled a can from its plastic loop, popped the tab
and drank. Dewey had thought to save the beer for home. "You
want me to drive?"

Russell laughed. The boy thought everything was funny.

Since they weren't moving, Dewey opened a can and took a
sip of beer. Anymore he hardly drank a thing. His heart, which
had always been sound, had recently gone bad. In some cases they
might ream out the arteries, the doctor said, but not with Dewey's
lungs being shot. He looked at the little old couple pictured on
the can label. The man looked like Dewey had expected to look
when he was a grandfather taking Mickey's kids to the zoo.

"When I was a boy we got squirrels in the fall. My father
roasted them in a covered pan, basted with blackberry brandy.
It made them dark as tar." He clucked his tongue. "You never
tasted a thing any sweeter."

Russell grunted.

Dewey fished out a Lucky and saw the boy's eyes flick to the
pack. He put the cigarettes on the blanketed seat between his
leg and the door. At heart he was not a selfish man. It put him
out of sorts to have not to offer the boy a smoke, but you started
in offering things to Russell and before you knew it he ended
up with everything you had.

"You wanna cross over here, come in the other side of the
river?"

"I wouldn't mind," Dewey said. The east bank roads were

twisty and narrow with few houses and no carryouts, the way River Road had been when he was a boy.

"Long as we don't run out of gas."

"I'm keeping an eye on it, I said."

Russell opened a second can and backed the truck. He held the beer in his left hand, letting go of the steering wheel with his right to shift quickly, then grab on again. The boy was hazardous in his lack of common sense. The Luv lurched forward, tires chucking gravel. Beer slopped onto Dewey's shirt. He blotted the spot with his handkerchief, but it would smell.

"Got an extra smoke?"

"Then you'd need three hands."

"Shh!"

Dewey knew what Russell meant to say. He'd told the boy straight out that he didn't care for foul language.

Dewey blew smoke through his nostrils. "We barked them using a .22 rifle. You had to hit the branch right beneath them. It stops the heart and you don't tear 'em up. Not much meat to those little fellas."

"I'd like to see somebody try that."

"You had to be a good shot."

"I heard guys say that," Russell said, "but never did believe it."

"Well, I'm here to tell you."

"Twenty gauge is what you need."

"Tears 'em up."

"A .22, you'd miss."

Dewey turned to face Russell. "I'm telling you we did it. Many's the time."

"You say so."

The wet road rushed past beneath Dewey's feet, spray from the tires hissing. "Your floorboards are rusted out," he said. "Somebody's going to fall right through there someday."

"A piece of crap, but what can I get? The rent, the electric. Shh."

"It's hard. Especially getting married so young."

When Mickey first started bringing Russell to the house,

Dewey'd tried to talk to him. Russell had nothing to say about football or baseball. You play anything in high school? Dewey asked. Poker, Russell said. Mickey and Margaret had a laugh at that. Everybody seemed to think Russell was Bob Hope.

"Not knockin Michelle. She's okay."

"She's a good girl," Dewey said. "Of course I wanted a boy. But I can't say I have any complaints about Mickey."

He watched the passing river. The Olentangy was high from runoff and turned the color of coffee with cream. It had been higher still that spring when they'd let water out of the reservoir. In trees angled over the banks dead limbs were snagged, turned sideways to the current and hanging a foot above the level of the river. A wad of trash was stuck in the crotch of a young syca-more. Toilet paper, Dewey saw, a length of it hanging down, fluttering in the cool air just above the water. At least the rains carried away some of the trash. Anymore people tossed things from their cars with no thought at all for their neighbor. Columbus people mostly, out to see the countryside.

"Guy I know works at the carnival."

The boy was eyeing Dewey with what appeared to be serious-ness. Even so, his rabbity teeth showed. Russell always looked to be laughing at things. Dewey had taken out a loan to have Mickey's teeth fixed when she was in junior high. It was more than he could afford but he figured it would be worth it.

"He said maybe he could get me in."

"A carnival?" Dewey said.

"Runnin the ferris wheel. Don't sound so bad."

"That Honda plant's going in over to Marysville."

"Work for Japs?"

"They're the ones hiring."

"This guy I know, he says Michelle could get something at a stand, pizza-burger. Both of us workin, we could put something aside."

"You get a lot of trash hanging around those outfits."

Russell looked like he might say something, then sucked at his beer.

"You ought not to drink while you're driving," Dewey said, finally.

Russell turned off River Road onto Home Road. After crossing the steel bridge, he parked on the berm. "We in any hurry?"

Dewey shook his head. He knew, as Margaret was always saying, that he had to meet Russell halfway. The thing of it was that Russell seemed to have no idea where his half started. Dewey opened a second can of Old Dutch. He didn't much care for beer, but thought to keep Russell from drinking it all. "We don't want to fill up. They'll be putting out a spread."

"You can't fill me up."

Russell had parked the Luv under the overhang of a big maple. Dewey listened to the dripping of the night's rain from the leaves onto the roof. A drop, then another, ran down the bug-spattered windshield. Across Home Road birds whistled and called in a field of hip-high corn. Through the field at an angle to the road marched giant power line pylons, like Martians.

Russell tapped the rim of his can against his teeth. "Guess I'll take the unemployment first. Twenty-six weeks, don't I get?"

Dewey didn't know what the boy had coming.

"Sometimes you get more, I gotta check on it. I thought you'd know."

"I'd like to help you, but I have no idea."

"What is it you're gettin?"

It took Dewey a moment to understand the question. He smacked his lips at the boy's stupidity. "You mean my disability? I get disability, such as it is."

"Yeah, I guess I can't get that."

"Sure you can," Dewey said. "Just work twenty years blowing in fiberglass and shoot your lungs all to heck. Then they give it to you for free."

Russell finished his beer. He opened the last can. After he'd put his mouth to it, he looked sidelong at Dewey. "You didn't want this, did you?"

Dewey guessed it was not his place to lecture Russell. The boy's father had been killed in a truck wreck before Russell was born. His mother was no good, which everybody knew. Loose Lucy. Maybe she'd done her best but a boy needed a man around and there wasn't any for Russell. Or too many. Same difference, come down to it. It was a sad thing. But it was too late for Dewey to teach Russell the things he ought to have learned growing up. He'd made a stab at it when Mickey first brought the boy to the house. Russell had made it plain it wasn't a daddy he'd come looking for.

Not that Dewey didn't try getting along with the boy. He told Margaret that. The thing of it was you couldn't talk to Russell. Margaret said it took time. But it was more than that, Dewey told her, he just didn't like the boy. He thought Mickey ought to have done better. What'd they spend all that money on piano lessons for? And the braces? Margaret said she wished she'd never said a thing to him about the kids' trouble.

Mickey had told Margaret but had made her promise not to tell Dewey about Russell pushing her down the apartment stairs. She said later, Margaret said, that Russell hadn't meant to. He slapped at Mickey and what with the basket of wet wash she couldn't catch herself. Nobody got hurt, anyhow. Dewey had kept his word, saying nothing to anyone, but it rankled. What was a father for? he wanted to know. If he was going to go on like that, Margaret said, then she wouldn't tell him anything anymore.

"They got trailers you can stay in. Maybe I'll take Michelle when the carnival comes around, see what she thinks."

"County fairs," Dewey said.

"We'd get to see some places. Better'n sittin around here."

"I don't see what's so awful about Olentangy. You were born and raised here, same as Mickey."

"Yeah, well. I don't wanna get stuck here all my life."

"You don't?" Dewey said with some surprise.

"Well, hell man! Not if I can't find any goddamn work!"

"You ought to watch your temper," Dewey said. "You're too hotheaded." There was more to be said but he did not trust his own temper. He left the truck. He smoked a Lucky and watched the smooth brown flow of the river.

Russell walked around to stand beside Dewey. He flipped his empty can into the water. The can bobbed, righted itself, and floated south.

"The damn mill shuttin down. What am I supposed to do?"

Even in the open air Dewey picked up the smell, a sugary spoilage.

"Lighthill himself told me it was sure to stay open."

Clint Lighthill, Russell's foreman, ex-foreman, had the same smell. Dewey and Clint had gone to high school together, Buck-eye Valley. Their senior year the Barons had been district runners-up. Clint was the halfback following Dewey into the hole.

"Old fart," Russell said, flashing his teeth.

"Clint worked there thirty years and more."

"He'll get retirement, won't he?" Russell seemed to be accusing Dewey of something.

"I would hope."

The boy nodded at the can in Dewey's hand. "You don't want that?"

"Don't rush me." Dewey tossed down his cigarette, ground it out, then worked on the warm beer. He did not like the dizziness beer caused him. When he was young he could drink all right. He figured now he did not get in enough air to offset the alcohol. Anymore his lungs had no more room in them than one of those little plastic coin purses. He dropped the empty can into the bed of the truck.

There were times when Dewey wondered what he might have done with his life if somebody had come up to him and plunked down a sum of money and said: "Dewey, you made a mistake. Insulation is not your line of work. We're going to give you another chance." He could have gone to mechanics school maybe. But that was not one of the things that happened to a man, though sometimes he might wonder about it. What happened mostly was hard luck. Dewey'd been forced to quit work just before the fuel oil shortage and home insulation boom. If he could have hung on he might have gone out on his own and gotten ahead of the game.

"The women are expecting us," he said. "Margaret made a potato salad. We might stop and pick up some pretzels."

"We better get some beer."

"I expect Margaret will give me an eight track. I have everything Benny Goodman ever did. She writes out a little card with the date and happy whatever. You get older, you come to appreciate that sort of thing in a woman."

Russell glanced at Dewey in what looked like embarrassment. On the other hand it could have been boredom.

It was hard for Dewey to see what Mickey saw in Russell. He had been her first boyfriend. Dewey had expected the thing to run its course and that to be an end to it.

"Another thing, you get older. You get to talking too much." Dewey smiled. "I recall my father doing that when he got up in years. Well, it didn't do anybody any harm."

"You're lucky you had a daddy."

"Yes, that's true. He taught me any number of things. How to drive and how to work with tools. How to handle a rifle and shotgun. He was a fine shot, a hard worker, all his life."

Russell's face brightened. "Let's shoot the cans."

"With what?"

Russell went around the truck to dig out a black thing from behind the driver's seat. It looked like a fishing tackle box. Dewey watched the boy unscrew a length of pipe from the plastic case and saw that it was a rifle barrel. Russell attached the barrel, action, and magazine to the hollow stock.

"Somethin, huh? Survival rifle, AR-7."

"You ought not to be carrying that thing around."

"Got it from the catalogue."

"That could get you in trouble."

"Got it in case of trouble," Russell said. He loaded the rifle. "Get the cans, okay?"

"We don't want to be gone too long." Dewey gathered the empties and followed Russell down to the river. His tan hush puppies were fairly new and he took care to step clear of mud. "Myself, I wouldn't be buying guns when I had no idea how I was to make a living."

"Season before last," Russell said, "I got a deer. Doe. Knocked her flat with a shotgun slug. Hit her in the heart."

"You dress it out?"

"Well, first shot tore up the gut. But I figure I get one this season, we could use the meat. Maybe put it in your freezer."

"Thing of it is," Dewey said, "Margaret stocks up, freezing vegetables. You and Mickey ought to think about a garden yourself."

"No place." Russell twitched his upper lip. "No freezer."

"Too late anymore this year. Next spring you might give it a try."

Russell stripped off his army shirt.

"Don't be waving that thing around," Dewey cautioned him.

"We could bet, you want to. Who gets the most hits."

"Always somebody getting hurt, you read about it in the papers."

Russell draped his shirt over a branch. He was pale and hairless but not skinny when you saw him up close, more stringy-muscled. Dewey realized with some surprise that the boy might whip him in a fair fight. He could recall a time when he wouldn't have thought twice about smacking down a punk like Russell.

"Couple bucks, what d'you say?"

"No," Dewey said.

"Say a six-pack, Rolling Rock."

"I'm not a betting man."

Russell sighed and rolled his eyes skyward. He took a can and tossed it into the river. Quickly he snapped the rifle to his shoulder and triggered off two shots, then a third. The rifle was a .22 semi-automatic. It must have cost near a hundred dollars. Dewey watched the riddled can sink.

"Bet you're glad you didn't bet."

"The river doesn't need our trash," Dewey said. "Line them up on that downed limb. We'll pick up after us when we're done." He handed the boy the four cans and took the rifle. It felt like a toy. He let it hang by his side, muzzle to the ground.

Russell put a can on the branch. It fell off, and again, and he called it a bitch, his voice low. Finally it stayed put.

"Mickey said you two had some trouble."

The boy looked up to Dewey, then back to the cans.

Dewey repeated his remark but Russell took no notice. Dewey breathed with his mouth open. It was muggy under the trees. The wet ground sucked at his shoes. Margaret had told him that Mickey had told her that she wasn't going to tell Russell about the baby. Not yet. Not with the mill closing. When things looked up she was sure he'd feel different about it. Margaret said she thought Mickey was probably right. She thought Russell had learned his lesson after that business on the stairs, she told Dewey.

Russell got the cans to stand in line.

"You ought to take better care of her," Dewey said.

"What?"

"You heard me. Mickey." Dewey brought the rifle to port position.

"Hey, man," Russell said, with what looked like fear on his face, or maybe anger. "Don't screw around, okay?"

"Did you hear me or not?"

"Yeah." The boy held his look, his mouth working, then looked down. "Okay, I heard you. Okay?"

After a moment Dewey said "All right," as if agreeing to something, though to what he didn't know. Russell looked up, then started briskly up the slope, his knobby shoulders squared like he had it in mind to teach the old fart a thing or two.

Dewey switched his hold to grip the rifle like a baseball bat. He took a backward step, swung hard, and let loose. Russell ducked. The .22 sailed in an arc, making one complete turn, and hit in the middle of the river. Russell spun about and let out a yelp like a boy catching his dingus in his zipper. Then he turned on Dewey. "Goddamnit! You crazy or something?"

The boy's look was so hot with accusation that Dewey could not begin to explain his good intentions. He shook his head, expressing his confusion, and saw as he did so that Russell took the gesture as one of apology.

"Yeah," the boy said. "So who's gonna get it?"

The rifle was floating, Dewey saw. He supposed that was the reason for the hollow stock, so you might take it fishing with you.

"Shoot!" Russell ran down to the river and waded in.

"You're a fool," Dewey said. "You'll drown."

Every year you read about somebody drowning in the Olentangy. It looked so flat and placid, so local, yet its hidden currents could drag the strongest man down.

When he was waist-deep, Russell lifted his arms over his head, then jumped or fell forward into the water. There was a smacking sound and white splash and he went under.

Go on down with the rest of the trash, Dewey said to himself.

Steadied by the submerged barrel, the plastic butt floated calmly on the surface. Suddenly Russell came up. He slapped and kicked at the water as though fighting his way out of a collapsed tent. He had none of the natural grace of a good swimmer. In the county pool Margaret scarcely left a wake and looked to be moving slow until you tried keeping up with her. The boy was going with the current though, and each smacking stroke closed the distance between him and the rifle. He opened his mouth wide, like a hooked bass, then closed it and went under. When he surfaced again he had the rifle. He turned sideways to the current and churned the water with one arm.

Dewey tripped on a root. He caught himself against a leaning tree. Without thinking to, he'd been walking downstream. He looked back and was surprised at how far he had come.

Aiming for the bank, Russell went under, came up, went under again. The boy wasn't going to make it, Dewey saw. He thought to shout something, but couldn't think of what. A phrase spray-painted on the railroad overpass near his house came to mind: third time's the charm. He'd suspected it had to do with teenagers and sex, but now thought it might mean drowning. "Drop it," he heard himself say. "Let it go."

The boy's arms flailed about. His white headband was gone and his hair flew. The wedge of black plastic separated from him then, bobbing wildly in his wake, and slowly he began making his way toward land.

Dewey walked quickly to a point at which he estimated the boy would strike the bank. He looked about, found a fallen limb, and pulled it free of weeds matted by higher water. It was twice as long as he was tall. The broken-off end as thick as his arm, it tapered to a tip no bigger than his little finger. He lifted it and brought it in a sidelong whipping motion, like a fly rod, to smack against the surface of the river. The boy's strokes slowed. The current would carry him past Dewey's station, out of reach. Lips pursed in disgust, Dewey stepped into the water, ruining his shoes. The bottom was slippery. He moved one step at a time, first probing with a toe, then planting a heel. The running brown water rose to his knees, then to his crotch. It was not what he would call cold, yet he felt his testicles tuck up, and he shivered. When he lifted the limb, the movement set him to dancing to regain his balance. He settled for poking it out as far as he could. The current tugged it south and he had to keep jerking it up and back like sweeping an oar.

Russell, his face white, slapped at the branch, caught it, and pulled. Dewey was jerked, stumbling, forward. The water rose to his waist and fear sent a jolt into his heart. He caught and held his ground. The boy slid slowly past him. Dewey walked backward, Russell a heavy drag at the end of the branch, until he reached the bank. Dewey sagged, and sat on a rock. He was breathing rapidly and shallowly, pains stabbing his arm and chest. His slacks stunk of river water and his shoes were slick with muck. Spots of light danced before his eyes.

The boy lay face down on the bank. His feet were still in the water and his bony shoulders shook with a rough, coughing sound. Dewey thought to kneel on Russell and pump water from him, but recognized then that the sound was not that of choking. He hawked, and spat. When the boy had quieted, finally, Dewey helped him to his feet. He kept his face turned away from Russell's; it embarrassed him to see fear in a man's eyes. Draping the boy's arm over his shoulders, he walked him halfway back to the truck before Russell pulled free. The boy went the rest of the way under his own power.

Russell leaned against the cab, his legs trembling like a dog's. Dewey got his Luckies out of the truck and saw that his own hands were not all that steady. You did a thing and maybe were all right at the time but later it hit you how close it had been. That was when you got the shakes. Then you started to feel numb, the sort of feeling a man has after he has taken a hard blow. Getting a cigarette lit, Dewey sucked in the hot dry smoke. It set him to coughing. When he'd caught his breath again, he stuck a Lucky between Russell's lips and lit it for him. The boy's wet hair hung down as long as a girl's. Dewey pulled the pink spread off the truck seat, the fabric covers were a disgrace of grease and holes, and draped it about Russell's shoulders. "I'll drive," he said. He held out his hand for the keys and the boy handed them over.

In town Dewey stopped at the Sohio self-serve and pumped five dollars of unleaded regular into the pickup's tank. When he got back into the cab, Russell didn't say a thing. He hadn't said thank you for being pulled from the river either, but Dewey let it pass.

The Matador was in the drive and Mickey was in the side yard kneeling by Margaret's flower bed. Dewey parked the Luv in front of the house. Russell shrugged off the blanket and got out the second the truck stopped. Dewey stayed behind the wheel to light another Lucky. Neither of them had said a thing about the rifle, but the boy ought to know there was no question but that Dewey would make it up to him. Mickey could use the money for groceries.

He watched Russell walk up the drive. Mickey looked up in surprise, then alarm, and rose to throw her arms around the boy's skinny neck. You'd never know to look at her that she was carrying a baby.

Dewey killed the engine, stepped into the street and ground out his cigarette. The hush puppies squished with water; he'd put them in the bag for Goodwill. Margaret opened the front door and looked out. When he saw her like that, without expecting to, he saw that she'd gotten to be a fat woman. Otherwise, he never thought of her that way. That must be the way other people saw her though. What they might think of him, he had no idea. He went up the three concrete steps to the porch with its love seat swing and blue-painted milk can.

"Wait!" Margaret called to him, and hurried away. When she came back, she was holding something bright and silvery in her hands, and he saw that it was his present.

ROBERT FLANAGAN was born in Toledo, Ohio, in 1941. He served in the Marine Corps Reserve, and graduated from the Universities of Toledo and Chicago. He has received a National Endowment for the Arts fellowship and three Ohio Arts Council grants, and has published a novel, *Maggot*. Mr. Flanagan lives in Delaware, Ohio, with his wife and two daughters, and teaches writing at Ohio Wesleyan University.